"Can you help me out of this shirt?"

Can't you just sleep in it? she wanted to ask. Helping him put it on had been intimate enough. Taking it off…

She was about to straight‍‍‍‍‍‍‍‍‍‍‍‍‍‍‍om when his finge‍‍‍‍‍‍‍‍‍‍‍‍‍up into her hair, aroun‍‍‍‍‍‍‍‍‍‍‍‍‍loser.

Before she coul‍‍‍‍‍‍‍‍‍‍‍‍mouth touched ‍‍‍‍‍‍‍‍‍‍‍‍essure, lips against lips, a pla‍‍‍‍‍‍‍‍. Then his tongue levered between her lips, dipping into her mouth, and her knees damn near gave way. There was no hurry, no desperation or need, just wanting. He wasn't going to die without her, or starve, or burst into flames.

No, the dying/starving/flame-bursting was all hers.

When he released her, his eyes remained closed. "Damn" was all he said, a hint of all his years in Texas creeping into the word, making it twice as long.

Yeah. *Damn.*

★★★

Dear Reader,

I've loved every book I've ever written and feel a great fondness for every couple that peopled them, but something about AJ Decker and Masiela Leal just grabbed me and wouldn't let go. I can't tell you why. They're smart and capable and mature—but so are my other heroes and heroines. They're flawed and human—but so are the others. They've suffered some deep hurts—but so have... Well, you get the idea.

Maybe it's because Decker is a cop, like my husband. Maybe because he has a deep sense of honor, like my father. Or maybe his hardheadedness reminds me of my son. And Mas—she's a strong woman, not just physically but in every other way. Like my mom, my sisters, my best friends. Like me.

Whatever the reason, I loved every moment I spent in Decker's and Mas's company, and I hope you do, too!

Marilyn

MARILYN PAPPANO

Protector's Temptation

ROMANTIC
SUSPENSE

SILHOUETTE BOOKS

Recycling programs for this product may not exist in your area.

ISBN-13: 978-0-373-27695-0

PROTECTOR'S TEMPTATION

Books by Marilyn Pappano

Silhouette Romantic Suspense

*Michael's Gift #583
*Regarding Remy #609
*A Man Like Smith #626
Survive the Night #703
Discovered: Daddy #746
*Convincing Jamey #812
*The Taming of
    Reid Donovan #824
*Knight Errant #836
The Overnight Alibi #848
Murphy's Law #901
**Cattleman's Promise #925
**The Horseman's Bride #957
**Rogue's Reform #1003
Who Do You Love? #1033
  "A Little Bit Dangerous"
My Secret Valentine #1053
**The Sheriff's Surrender #1069
The Princess and
  the Mercenary #1130
**Lawman's Redemption #1159
**One True Thing #1280
**The Bluest Eyes in Texas #1391

Somebody's Hero #1427
More Than a Hero #1453
One Stormy Night #1471
Forbidden Stranger #1495
Intimate Enemy #1529
Scandal in Copper Lake #1547
Passion to Die For #1579
Criminal Deception #1591
Protector's Temptation #1625

*Southern Knights
**Heartbreak Canyon

MARILYN PAPPANO

has spent most of her life growing into the person she was meant to be, but isn't there yet. She's been blessed with family—her husband, their son, his lovely wife and a grandson who is almost certainly the most beautiful and talented baby in the world—and friends, along with a writing career that's made her one of the luckiest people around. Her passions, besides those already listed, include the pack of wild dogs who make their home in her house, fighting the good fight against the weeds that make up her yard, killing the creepy-crawlies that slither out of those weeds and, of course, anything having to do with books.

Chapter 1

The blow was sharp and unexpected. An elbow slammed AJ Decker in the gut, followed by a bite to his left hand. His grunt bit off into a curse, drowned out by a shout from the uniformed officer hustling around the car.

"Watch out, Lieutenant! Willie likes to go for the—!"

The warning faded as the prisoner, hands still cuffed, kicked out with regrettable accuracy. Blood drained from AJ's face, and little more than a huff of breath escaped him as he sank to the ground on hands and knees. Pain washed up in waves, creating a roaring in his ears that reduced the pounding of feet and the struggle between prisoner and officers to a distant rumble. Oh, God, he was going to be sick.

Gritting his teeth, he willed the nausea away. He would never live this down—the growing crowd of witnesses spilling out of the police department confirmed that—but damned if he'd make an embarrassing situation worse by puking up his guts in front of the whole damn department.

AJ's vision cleared as three or four officers dragged Willie away kicking and screaming obscenities, and he focused on a hand stuck out to him. He took it, and Tommy Maricci, one of the detectives who worked for him, pulled him to his feet. Maricci was trying hard not to grin when he let go.

"Rule one in dealing with Willie Franklin—always protect your nads," Maricci said mildly.

"I've never dealt with Willie Franklin before." AJ's voice was reasonably strangled, since even the shallowest of breaths hurt deep inside. "Please God, I never will again."

The officer who'd been bringing Willie in for booking—thirty pounds over department fitness guidelines and two years short of retirement—reluctantly approached. His cheeks were red, and sweat gleamed on his forehead. "I should've warned you sooner, Lieutenant, but I just figured everyone knew you don't give Willie a chance to kick."

"Yeah, well, *now* everyone knows." AJ straightened to his full height, then sucked in a pain-filled breath. He'd managed to reach the age of thirty-eight without ever taking a hit to the testicles, but now he understood why guys who did curled into the fetal position. It hurt. Like hell.

As his audience drifted back inside the building, he took a tentative step, then another, grinding his teeth against the throb. He wasn't sure he would ever walk normally again. He managed a few more steps before a voice cutting through the warm afternoon brought him up short.

"Jeez, Decker. Brought down by a woman—and a scrawny one at that. You're slipping."

Slowly he turned, staring at the owner of the voice. The man stood on the curb ten feet away, wearing a gray suit, a lighter gray shirt and a burgundy tie. He looked as if he could be on his way to court, except for the lack of a briefcase…and the fact that the courtrooms where he prosecuted cases for the State of Texas were nowhere near Copper Lake, Georgia.

"Scrawny women are usually the dirtiest fighters," AJ replied evenly before extending his hand. "Donovan. What the hell are you doing here?"

Ray Donovan closed the distance between them, shaking hands. "Looking for you."

That couldn't be good news. They'd been friendly enough back in Texas, but not really buddies. It had been their jobs that brought them together: AJ had been a homicide detective with the Dallas PD and Donovan had been an assistant district attorney. You catch 'em, I'll clean 'em and we'll let the state fry 'em, he used to joke. They'd done just that often enough.

AJ drew a careful breath and decided he might live after all. "Ray Donovan, Tommy Maricci." He didn't bother with any further introduction. Donovan had probably already noticed the badge clipped to Maricci's belt, and any cop as good as Maricci recognized a prosecutor when he saw one.

The two men shook hands, then Donovan gestured toward a bench shaded by an overgrown crape myrtle. "I'd ask you to take a walk, but since you probably wouldn't make it to the curb, can we talk over there?"

Maricci snickered as AJ scowled. The hell of it was, Donovan was right. He wasn't going to be moving too fast or too far for a while.

"I'll give Wilhelmina your best," Maricci said, slapping AJ on the back before he headed into the police station.

Hiding a wince, AJ limped the ten feet to the wrought-iron bench and gingerly eased down. Damn. Sitting was no more comfortable than standing. Lying down—after guzzling half a bottle of whiskey—was the only thing that was going to make him feel better.

Donovan didn't sit but stood gazing into the distance.

When he didn't speak, AJ did. "You ever get out of that suit?"

Donovan's gaze flickered over him. "You're not my type."

AJ snorted. He knew Donovan's type too well. How many women had he dated in Dallas who'd dropped him for Donovan? Two? No, three, counting the cheerleader.

They could make small talk until Donovan was ready, but AJ wasn't very good at small talk, so he went straight to the point. "What do you want with me?"

"An old case came across my desk a few weeks ago. A pimp convicted of killing one of his girls. Got a life sentence. His lawyer didn't like the verdict and wouldn't leave it alone. She kept poking around, asking questions, reviewing statements. Now she thinks she's uncovered some serious problems with the investigation."

"What do you think?"

Donovan's smile was rueful. "I'd like to believe she's wrong. I prosecuted the case. Sending the wrong man to prison doesn't look good on my record. But based on what I've seen so far, she might be right."

"You think he's innocent?" AJ asked.

"Not by a long shot. But he might be innocent of this particular crime."

"What does any of this have to do with me?"

Donovan glanced toward the parking lot, where patrol cars were pulling in for shift change, then lowered his gaze to the ground. "Since word got out that we were taking another look at the case, she's gotten some threats. Someone took a shot at her. Someone broke in to her house. They've left messages and notes warning her to drop it."

Which meant she was probably right. Still, Dallas was a long way outside AJ's jurisdiction. He wasn't with DPD anymore. He hadn't stayed in touch with anyone once he'd left. Donovan's story was vaguely interesting, but there was no reason for him to be telling it now, unless AJ had worked the case, which he hadn't. He remembered every homicide case he'd ever worked, and none had involved a pimp and one of his girls.

"What does this have to do with me?" he asked again.

Still staring down, Donovan traced a crack in the pavement with the toe of his shoe before looking up hesitantly. AJ was surprised. He'd never seen Donovan anything less than supremely confident.

"I'm looking for a place to put the lawyer for a few days. I don't want anything to happen to her while I go over her information."

For a moment AJ looked blankly at him, then Donovan's meaning penetrated. "You want to bring her here? To Copper Lake?" He snorted. "Come on, Donovan, the State of Texas can do better than this. You can set up a safe house almost anywhere. You've got the entire DPD to help you out, and if they're not enough, there's the Rangers and the feds."

Again, Donovan avoided his gaze for a moment before sighing heavily. "I don't know who I can trust in Texas. The guys who threatened her, who shot at her and broke into her house...we have reason to believe they're cops."

Damn. "Dallas cops?"

Donovan nodded. The state didn't pay him anywhere near what he was worth, but he had family money. He didn't need the salary. That helped make him a hell of a prosecutor: he couldn't be bought.

AJ didn't have family money, but he couldn't be bought, either. Though he'd run across plenty of people who could.

Easing to his feet, AJ grimaced at the discomfort that intensified before settling into a dull throb. He wasn't naïve. Cops were like any other professionals: some good, some bad, some indifferent. Some were tempted by power, by greed, by ego. The good ones outnumbered the bad a hundred to one, but it only took one to taint an entire department.

"So you're requesting the assistance of the Copper Lake Police Department." AJ shook his head. Big city coming to the small town for help. Who would have believed it?

"No, actually, I'm requesting *your* assistance. I'd like to put her up with you for a while. The fewer people who know, the better."

"Why me?"

"Because I can trust you. You'd never be tempted by money or brotherhood or friendship. You do what's right."

Strict moral code. That was what AJ's dad called it. Right and wrong, good and bad were concepts Adam Decker lived by. He'd never wavered, even when it would have been easy, even when it would have profited him. AJ had done his best to do the same.

He walked a few feet, his gaze on the traffic on Carolina Avenue. Copper Lake was your average small town: twenty-thousand people, relatively pleasant, relatively safe. The population covered the spectrum of race and social and economic status, with an average ratio of criminals to law-abiding citizens and those skirting the edge. It wasn't the kind of place anyone would expect a homicide detective from Dallas to choose.

Or a defense attorney in hiding.

Then something Donovan had said echoed in his head. *You'd never be tempted by...brotherhood or friendship.* Abruptly he turned back. "I know these cops?"

Donovan nodded.

"Who are they?"

"Your old running buddies from Homicide. Myers. Taylor. Kinney."

Muscles tightening, AJ got a really bad feeling in his gut. He looked at the parking lot, scanning for a car that didn't belong, and found it in a black sedan with tinted windows and a lone figure sitting in the passenger seat. From this distance, and with the tint, it was impossible to make out anything about her, but he knew pretty much all he needed to.

Heat rose into his face, carrying with it anger that he'd thought he'd put behind him years ago. He scowled at Donovan. "This is about the Riggs case, isn't it? Teri Riggs. Israel Rodriguez. And *her.*" He stabbed a finger in the direction of the car. "You brought her here, expecting me to take her in, let her stay at my house, keep an eye on her? You're nuts!"

Donovan dragged his fingers through his hair. If AJ's was long enough, he'd be tearing it out. "I brought her here because I know that case is important to you. You of all people would want to be sure that the man in prison for Riggs's murder was the one who actually killed her. I know you two—" his gesture toward the car showed agitation, a rare thing in a hotshot prosecutor "—have a history. But she trusts you, and so do I. There aren't many people capable of protecting her that we can say that about."

Before AJ could repeat his last words, Donovan went on. "Look, you're off work now, right? Can we go to your house and talk about this, all three of us?

"You can go back to whatever the hell airport you came in at and go home. I don't want a damn thing to do with it." AJ spun around, wincing, and headed for the building fifteen feet away. He would clear his desk, go home, get an ice pack and a cold beer, then sack out on the couch and do his best to forget how crappy this afternoon had turned out.

But he'd gone less than five feet when another voice spoke. "Hey, bitch, you know what's good for you, you'll mind your own business. If you don't, whatever happens, it's all on you."

Slowly he turned back.

Donovan was holding a small tape recorder. "You know that voice."

AJ wanted to deny it, but he didn't waste his breath. "Yeah." Dave Kinney, former fellow homicide detective, an overall decent guy who cut a few corners but always for the better good. It was not only his voice, but the final words—*it's all on you*—were a favorite phrase of his.

"Can we talk at your house?"

It took a moment to force the words out, but AJ managed. "Give me five minutes. You can follow me there."

* * *

Masiela Leal sat in the car, steadfastly refusing to watch the conversation between Decker and Donovan. When Donovan had pulled into the parking lot, she'd caught a glimpse of Decker on his way to the patrol unit parked at the curb, and that glimpse had hurt, God, so much more than she'd expected. All the time since, she'd looked anywhere, everywhere, but at him.

This was a bad idea. True, she hadn't felt safe anywhere in Texas—not at her condo in Dallas, her sister's house in Austin or her brother's apartment in Houston. As a former cop, she knew too well how cops stuck together. If you were a part of the brotherhood, it could be a wonderful thing. If you weren't, it could be damned scary.

And she'd been scared since that first phone call.

The driver's door lock clicked, and an instant later, Donovan slid into the seat.

"Let me guess," she said as he buckled his seat belt. "He wasn't overjoyed to hear my name."

Donovan flashed her a rueful smile. "I didn't even have to *say* your name. But we're going to his house, so that's something." He sounded tired, as if he'd just put on the best closing argument of his career.

And he must have, if Decker had agreed to let her set foot inside his house.

Donovan added reassurance. "I still think this is the best place for you."

Who do you trust? he had asked after the gunshot that shattered the office window she had been gazing from. She hadn't even needed to think about it. The one person she'd ever trusted one hundred percent was her ex-partner and friend, no matter that the friendship had been over for a long time. He was as willing to risk his life for a scumbag in protective custody as he was for a fellow officer. His feelings for you, good or bad, had nothing to do with it. It was his feelings for himself that counted. He had a code of honor, and by God, he lived by it.

Instead of answering the question, she'd turned it back on him, and he'd given the same answer she would have: AJ Decker.

"What do you think of the town?" Donovan asked as he started the engine. "Think you can manage here for a week or so?"

"It's not a cave in the woods, but it'll do." Masiela knew from Donovan's action that Decker must be ready to leave, but she resisted the urge to turn around and look for him. She would have to face him soon enough.

A big white pickup passed behind them, and Donovan backed out, then trailed it to the street. All she could see of Decker was the back of his head and his broad shoulders. He was still keeping his head damn near shaved, she noted bittersweetly, and she would bet he still looked damn good that way.

They followed him through downtown Copper Lake, then a neighborhood with grand old homes, into blocks with smaller houses. When Decker turned into the driveway of one, she was momentarily surprised. He'd always preferred apartments in Dallas—didn't want the maintenance or expense of a house, didn't want nosy neighbors or noisy kids running around. Owning a house, he'd once told her, was the kind of commitment that followed marriage and babies, and he had no desire for either.

Oh, God, was he married now? Were there little Deckers running around Copper Lake? And what would a Mrs. Decker think of a woman from his past showing up in his present?

As Donovan shut off the engine and unfastened his seat belt, she bit back the impulse to tell him she'd changed her mind, that she'd rather take her chances in Dallas. Instead, she slowly climbed out, focusing narrowly on the house instead of the man climbing the steps.

It was Victorian in style, though lacking most of the frills. The colors were muted—peach, with cream trim and deep green accents, and the door was framed on top and both sides with stained glass. It was so *not* Decker that she was convinced he must have a wife who'd chosen this house.

And why shouldn't he have married? It had been six years since he'd left Dallas. People moved on. Their lives changed. And it wasn't as if there had been anything personal between the two of them.

Not on his part, at least.

Nothing that had extended past one night.

She and Donovan reached the bottom of the broad steps. The front door stood open, but there was no sign of Decker in the long hallway. She took a breath, forcing herself up each step, across the porch and inside the house. It smelled of wood and paint and dust, a fragrance explained when she stepped into the double doorway of the living room. Drop cloths covered the floor, bare studs were exposed and window and door casings were missing. A glance through another wide doorway showed the dining room in the same state. The house might be a showplace on the outside, but inside it was getting a whole new remodel.

Noise came from the back, and she and Donovan moved toward it. Decker was in the kitchen, getting a beer from the refrigerator. He popped the top off the bottle, took a swig, then leaned against the countertop and simply looked at both of them, no emotion whatsoever on his face.

She kept her arms limp at her sides. The most nervous she'd ever been in her life was the first time she'd faced a jury. She hadn't eaten anything all that day, for fear she wouldn't keep it down, and had still thrown up minutes before walking into the courtroom.

That was exactly what she wanted to do now, but she'd had a few years' experience since then in hiding her nerves. She smiled faintly and said, "Hello, Decker."

"Mas."

She'd always liked the way he said her name, all soft sounds in his gravel-rough voice: *mah-see-A-luh*. The fact that he'd used the nickname that belonged to only him and her family gave her brief hope that everything wasn't irrevocably ruined between them. The fact that he'd said it with an icy, hazel stare and all the warmth of a glacier kicked that hope back down.

A moment of uncomfortable silence settled, broken at last by Donovan. He went straight to the point. "Can I leave Masiela here with you?"

Decker continued to stare at her as if the sheer hostility in his look might reduce her to ash. "Rodriguez killed Teri."

He'd been convinced of that years ago, and Masiela had been just as convinced that he was opting for the easy choice. Better to believe that the abusive pimp had thrown Teri Riggs off a five-story building than that his cop buddies might be involved. But not all cops were as honest as Decker. The Brat Pack wasn't even as honest as the average criminals.

"Donovan has his doubts," she said evenly.

His gaze flickered to Donovan, then back again, but he didn't argue. He respected Donovan's judgment. He respected everyone's judgment except hers. Why? She'd been his partner for three years. He'd listened to her, asked for her opinion and advice. They'd worked well together. But when it counted, he'd dismissed her. *Why?*

He took another long drink. "I don't have time to babysit anyone."

"I don't need babysitting," she replied. "Just a place to stay, where Kinney and his buds won't find me."

"What makes you think I won't tell them you're here?"

The only answer she offered was a snort.

Though his gaze remained on her, AJ's next words were directed to Donovan. "You could just stick her in a motel somewhere."

"People would know. Clerks, housekeeping, pizza delivery guys. I don't want her under the radar. I want her off of it completely. And you have to admit, this little burg is pretty well off the radar."

After a long, stiff silence, AJ drained the beer, opened the cabinet under the sink and set the bottle inside a bin there. "A week. No longer."

Donovan looked relieved. Masiela felt it right down to her toes. Where she would go from there was anyone's guess, but for a week at least, she was safe. "I'll get her bags," Donovan said, leaving the kitchen before Decker could change his mind.

She rested one hand on the countertop, on a four-inch tile of milky green. It was cool and stilled the trembling in her fingers. "Do you need to clear this with anyone?"

"Like who?"

She shrugged. "Your wife?"

His gaze narrowed. "Don't have one."

So he'd chosen the Victorian all on his own. She would have smiled at the idea if he hadn't looked so forbidding.

Once he'd gotten the green light, Donovan was quick. He brought in her suitcases, gave Decker his cell phone number, issued a few warnings and was gone all in a matter of minutes. She listened to the front door close, followed by the sound of an engine revving, then silence.

"Well…" She sounded too cheery, too phony. "Can I put my stuff someplace?"

"My bedroom is the only one that's livable. You'll have to sleep here." Decker gestured to the other end of the room. "The couch folds out. There's a bathroom down the hall, but you'll have to shower upstairs."

She gazed at the space. Where a breakfast table and chairs should go, sat a brown leather sofa flanked by two stone-topped tables, with a longer matching table in front. Pushed against the opposite wall was a flat screen television on a steel-and-glass stand. Once the sofa was made into a bed, there would be just enough room to squeeze past both on the sides and at the foot.

So she'd traveled all those miles from Dallas to sleep on a fold-out in the corner of AJ Decker's kitchen. Wonderful. Not that she was complaining. The Brat Pack would never think to look for her here.

Her shoes echoing on black-and-white tile that looked original to the house, she carried her larger suitcase to the couch, opened it and removed her .40-caliber pistol from the top of a stack of shirts. She clipped the leather holster onto her waistband in back and immediately felt a hundred percent safer.

"How did you get a gun on the airplane?" Decker asked.

"We didn't fly commercial. Donovan's got his own plane. It makes it harder for anyone to track where he goes."

"You really think Kinney and the others killed Teri?"

She fixed her gaze on him. "Do you really think they're not capable?" They were considered good cops. They made a lot of arrests that resulted in a lot of convictions. But there had been whispers of impropriety for as long as she'd worked with them. Questions about how their success was achieved. Hints of wrongdoing.

"Of murder? No," Decker said flatly. "I don't believe it."

Loyal to his friends—maybe to a fault—but not loyal enough to her. If the victim had been someone other than Teri Riggs, if she had been a stranger to him, would he still have reacted the way he did? What role had grief and guilt played in forming his response?

"Then why the phone call?" Masiela asked. "I assume Donovan had to play the message to get your help." She saw by the slight shift in his expression that he had, indeed, heard the tape. "If everything in the case was by the book, why did Kinney find it necessary to threaten me?"

"Gee, I don't know. Maybe because you're screwing with his reputation. Because you have a knack for creating doubt where there isn't any." His sarcasm faded into flatness. "They put together a good case. The DA's office bought it. The jury bought it."

"They were wrong." The first time she'd argued for Rodriguez's innocence with Decker, she'd been fueled purely by instinct. This time she had evidence. Not that

Decker would ask to see it. If he did see it, he would be forced to set friendship aside, to acknowledge the ugly truth about his buddies.

"That's it, isn't it?" he challenged. "The jury believed the prosecution instead of you. You never could stand to lose."

She laughed. "Right. I became a defense attorney so I'd never have to face the possibility of losing." Sure, she had a competitive streak. She'd pushed herself hard to meet Decker and the other cops she'd worked with on their level, whether it was in the field, the interrogation room, the courtroom, the gym or the bar. It had been the only way to survive in their male-dominated field. But her ego wasn't so monstrous that losing threatened it.

"What I can't stand is my client sitting in prison for a crime he didn't commit. What I really can't stand are cops whose job is to uphold the law, who have a moral obligation to live to a higher standard, breaking that law for their own benefit. And I really, really can't stand cops who murder to keep their dirty activities secret. Who leave a little girl without a mother, without a home, without anyone who gives a damn."

Her last words struck a response, as she'd known they would. Teri Riggs had been a lot of things: prostitute, drug addict, petty thief, daughter, sister, lover. And her two most important roles: Decker's informant and Morgan's mother. The girl had been six when her mother died, a big-eyed waif surrounded by a sense of loss too huge for her to grasp. It had broken Decker's heart to see her at the funeral with no one but a social worker to turn to for comfort, and *that* had broken Masiela's heart.

His gaze darkened and a muscle twitched in his jaw,

but he didn't argue. Instead, after a moment, he turned and stiffly walked away.

Grateful for the reprieve, she sank onto the sofa, eyes closed, and let the trembling inside her run its course. This wasn't going to be easy. But as her grandmother used to say, "That which doesn't kill us makes us stronger."

She was going to be damn near invincible when she left here.

Chapter 2

Climbing the stairs was a slow and painful process, but AJ did it the way he did everything else—one dogged step at a time. When he reached the top, he allowed himself a grunt of relief, as much for the distance between him and Masiela as for reaching his goal. He passed two bedrooms that were currently serving as storage, and the remodeled bathroom that he'd finished just a week ago, to reach the master bedroom. It was the first room he'd tackled—his learning experience—and had taken way longer than it should have, but it had turned out okay. At least that was what Cate said the first time she'd slept over.

As he stripped off his clothes, he wondered what the good doctor would think if she found out about Masiela being here.

He hung up his jacket, tossed his shirt and trousers into the laundry hamper, then dressed in a paint-stained pair of denim shorts and an equally stained T-shirt. Given the choice, he would stretch out in bed for a while, but Dave Kinney had taken away that choice.

That damn fool. What had he been thinking, threatening Masiela on her answering machine? Even a rookie cop knew better than that. You never said anything on the record that could come back and bite you on the ass, and a recording was about as "on the record" as anything could get.

Granted, Kinney and the others had never been real fond of Masiela. They'd thought she didn't belong in homicide, that her promotion had been motivated more by race and gender than ability. They'd made it tough for her to fit in.

Not that she'd tried too hard. The cop job had been a temporary thing for her, something to pay the bills while she finished law school. As soon as she'd passed the bar, she'd quit the department and, adding insult to injury, she'd immediately begun defending the people they'd arrested.

Still, the threat had been stupid.

Unwilling to hide out in his room—actually, willing to do it but unwilling to admit to doing it—he made a stop at the linen closet in the hall, then gingerly went down the stairs again. Masiela was in the kitchen where he'd left her, now sitting on the sofa. If he could forget the years since she'd walked away from the department, there'd be a familiar, comfortable feel to the scene. They'd been partners and friends back then, and she'd spent as much time at his apartment as she had at home. But he wouldn't forget, even if he could.

He dumped the things he carried on the kitchen counter—two sheets, two blankets and a pillow—then gestured. "Make yourself at home." The invitation sounded as grudging as he felt. Hey, she had invited herself—or had Donovan do it for her—to be his guest. He didn't have to be gracious about it.

She nodded.

"Okay, here's the rules. You don't go anywhere, not even onto the porch. You stay out of sight. You don't answer the phone, you don't make any calls, you don't send any e-mails. Nobody's gonna know you're here."

She didn't roll her eyes, but she came close. "I told you: I don't need a babysitter. I'm not stupid, Decker. I understand the concept of hiding out."

"It's not my job to entertain you. And I don't want to hear—"

"The truth?"

His jaw tightened, sending an ache from his teeth up to the top of his skull. "I know those guys. We went through the academy together. Hell, Stan Myers saved my life."

Something flashed across her face. Regret, maybe. God knew, he had plenty of that. "You know me, too," she said quietly.

Not as well as he'd thought.

With the muscles in his neck knotting, he did the easiest thing: he retreated. It wasn't the same as hiding out, he told himself as he went through the dining room into the living room. Working on his house was what he did damn near every evening. It was his routine.

When he'd bought the house, his only experience with power tools had been watching his dad on the occasional woodworking project when he was a kid. He'd had the Internet for guidance, though, and Russ Calloway, owner of Copper Lake's biggest construction company, had been generous with advice.

The original walls had been plaster and lath in sorry

shape, so he was replacing them with wallboard, which his mother had offered to paint. Carol Ann lived to redecorate. His dad joked that every time he went out of town on business, he was afraid he wouldn't recognize the house when he got home. Both of them were happy she could decorate this house, instead of changing their own for the hundredth time. AJ figured it was a fair enough deal. He wasn't into paint or fabrics or accessories. On his own, he would paint the walls white and leave the windows and floors uncovered. If giving him something else satisfied his mom's creative urges, fine.

As he positioned a piece of wallboard against the front wall, footsteps came to a halt in the doorway. Though he refused to look at Masiela, all his other senses were hyperalert. He heard the even cadence of her breathing. He smelled the fragrance she'd always worn—subtle, teasing, spicy with a hint of sweetness. He felt the weight of her dark brown gaze measuring. The look had as much substance as a touch, making his muscles tighten.

Once the wallboard was in place, he braced it with one hand and his knee while picking up the nail gun at his feet. He shot two nails in at the top to secure it to the studs, then finished with another dozen nails before setting the tool down again.

"What changed your mind about buying a house?" she asked as he pulled another piece of Sheetrock from the stack against the far wall.

"It was a good deal." True as far as it went. The elderly woman who'd lived there had moved into a nursing home up in Raleigh, and her son, also in Raleigh, had wanted to unload the house quickly. AJ had had enough money in savings to make the payment no more than his monthly rent on an apartment half the size.

And he'd been thinking for a while that maybe it was time to settle down. To think about getting married and giving his parents a few of those grandkids they wanted so much.

Masiela wasn't put off by his brief answer. She moved farther into the room, crossing to the window seat of white pine and brushing away a coating of dust before seating herself. "It's not quite the place I would have pictured for you."

He sneaked a sidelong glance at her. Had she done that after he left Dallas—tried to picture him in new surroundings? Wondered what he was doing? Regretted what she'd done?

He'd thought about her for a while. Too long. It had taken a long time to get over missing her. To get past the point where his first thought when something happened to amuse or piss him off wasn't that she would get a kick out of it.

And here she was, back again. But he wouldn't make the same mistakes this time. He wouldn't think of her as a friend. He wouldn't forget that he couldn't trust her.

"I still have my condo," she said, though he hadn't asked. "I haven't been staying there for a while, though. Not since Kin—someone trashed it. I've spent the last two weeks in a different motel every night."

He checked the fit of the second piece of wallboard and put in a couple nails before asking, "You have proof?"

"No."

"Then you should know better than to slander someone, being a criminal defense attorney and all." He didn't have to look to know her mouth had flattened into a thin line. He'd seen it too many times when she was annoyed. When she finally responded, she would change the subject, and her voice would be cool enough to make the air-conditioning that had just kicked on unnecessary.

It was a few minutes in coming, but she proved him right. "When I heard you'd left to go back east, I figured Atlanta or Charlotte. Why Copper Lake?"

"They were hiring."

"And it's close to your parents."

He grunted.

"Do you like it?"

He scored a piece of wallboard, then broke it in two with a little more force than was needed. He wasn't socially stunted. He could carry on a conversation. He talked to people he'd rather not talk to all the time. And since he was going to have to talk to Masiela for the next week—because there was no way she'd be quiet for that long—he might as well get used to it and not give himself a headache.

"Yeah, I like it. It's different from Dallas."

"Not so much violent crime?"

"We have our share. But not so much that we need dedicated homicide, burglary or sex crimes squads. We just have the one detective division, and everyone works whatever comes up."

"And you're in charge."

"Yeah."

The air rustled as she shifted on the bench. "You always said you didn't want a supervisory position."

Where's your ambition? she'd teased. And his regular response: *I've achieved my only goal.* He'd wanted to do the work—investigate the crimes, follow the clues and arrest the bad guys. And through their whole time as partners, she'd intended to become another Donovan and prosecute them. They would still have been a team, just working in different offices.

Then she'd gone into criminal defense instead.

And she'd defended Israel Rodriguez.

"I didn't particularly want to be in charge," he said, grimly turning his thoughts away from the case that had ended everything between them. "But I had a hell of a lot more experience than anyone else in the department. It's not bad. I don't have to do too much supervising."

"So a big-city cop can be satisfied in a small town?"

"Why not? I've been here six years, and no one's taken a shot at me yet."

She made a soft *hmmph* sound. "I guess that counts for something. I can tell you from personal experience that getting shot at as a cop is a whole different thing than getting shot at as a lawyer."

AJ glanced at her over his shoulder. "You've got no proof of who did that, either, do you?" She represented scumbags for a living. Any one of them, or any one of the people they victimized, could have taken that shot.

"No," she agreed, sounding too cheerful. "Just gut instinct and common sense. And since you apparently don't believe I have either…"

Once he'd trusted her instincts as much as his own. If she'd said something didn't feel right, he'd *known* something *wasn't* right. But when she'd turned down a job offer from the DA's office to defend criminals instead, yeah, he'd lost his faith in both her instincts and her common sense.

Finally, he faced her head-on for the first time since she'd come into the room. "Look, I already told you, I don't want to talk about your so-called case. If you're going to stay here, if we're going to talk at all, change the subject."

Again her mouth thinned and her gaze locked on him. She'd hardly changed in the last six years. Her hair was still silky blue-black, falling straight past her shoulders and parted on one side, so that a few strands fell above her left eye. Her skin was still the color of dark, golden honey, her lips still full, her jaw still stubborn. She was still only five-five, slender and delicate, and still looked as if the only thing she could do with regards to cops was call one or be protected by one.

But the appearance was deceiving. Underneath that white T-shirt and the black jeans was muscle, courage and determination. She'd more than held her own against men twice her size. She could shoot better than most cops, had a fine appreciation for a Taser and could bring a three-hundred-pound Goliath to his knees with a simple wristlock. When they'd worked out together regularly, she could bench press her own weight and then some, and being shorter hadn't meant being slower when they went out for a run.

And underneath all *that,* she was all soft, delicate, enticing woman. He'd learned that for himself one night.

Had she ever remembered?

Would he ever forget?

Someday. He was sure of it. It just hadn't happened yet.

The Decker she'd worked with never would have been so dismissive of a threat, Masiela thought, stifling her sigh. If she were somebody else—or if the shooter had been somebody else—he would have at least been willing to hear her out. She would like to think that, maybe, if the bullet had found its target, he would show concern, but that could just be wishful thinking.

She'd done more than enough of that where Decker was concerned.

Change the subject, he'd said. Instead, as the nail gun fired again in rapid succession, she rose from the bench and returned to the kitchen. Taking his make-yourself-at-home invitation to heart, she opened the refrigerator and scanned its contents. Bottled water, pop, beer, condiments, margarine, two oranges and lettuce so old that it was growing something. The freezer held a bag of snack-size candy bars, a half-gallon tub of ice cream covered with rime and a stack of frozen dinners.

His aversion to cooking apparently hadn't changed, she noted drily, as she took a bottle of water, then closed both doors.

There was a window over the kitchen sink, and three of them behind the sofa, letting in the afternoon sun along with a fair amount of heat. Stay away from the windows, he'd warned her. These back windows posed no threat, since a heavily wooded area started where the yard ended.

She sat down on the sofa, the leather warm through her clothes, and reached for the remote to turn on the TV. But she wasn't much of a TV watcher, no matter what was going on in her life, and nothing on the fifty or so channels held her interest. Shutting off the sound, she sprawled out on the couch, a pillow stuffed beneath her head, and contemplated living a week in this dining-nook-turned-living-and-bedroom with her less than friendly host.

And a week was all Decker had given them—maybe enough time to review the files she'd given Donovan. Then he would probably take it to a grand jury, which would take more time, and they would have to hand down an indictment. She didn't know where she would go when she left Copper Lake—she and Donovan hadn't looked that far ahead—but one thing was sure: she couldn't return home until the Brat Pack were in custody.

She would be lucky if she hadn't gone insane by then.

It was six-thirty when Decker came into the room again. "I'm ordering pizza. Is that okay?"

"Sure."

He didn't ask what she wanted, but dialed the number. He probably didn't care.

But a moment later he surprised her when he placed the order: one large pie, thick crust and loaded, and the second, thin crust, vegetarian. He remembered, just as she remembered he liked sugar in his coffee, lemon in his tea and lime with his beer.

Except, *she* remembered because he—and his friendship—still meant something to her. *He* remembered because he had a great head for trivia.

When he hung up the phone, instead of returning to work, he got a beer, then eased onto one of the stools at the dining peninsula. He drank half of it before breaking his silence. "You ever see any of the old crew?"

She would like to say no, but she tried not to tell unnecessary lies. "Sure. In court on a regular basis."

"So you're still defending scum."

"Everyone's entitled to a lawyer." She knew his response before he gave it, because they'd had this discussion before, starting the day she'd turned down the DA's job offer.

"But that lawyer doesn't have to be you."

"Why shouldn't it be? I know the law. I know police procedure."

"And you know you're helping people who are guilty as sin walk out free."

Masiela didn't respond. She used her best judgment in deciding whether to take on a client. If she truly believed he was guilty, if the evidence was overwhelming, she sent him out the door. But reminding Decker of that wouldn't win her any points. Most of her clients were guilty of something—maybe not the crime they'd been charged with, but *something*. Israel Rodriguez had beaten his girls, along with the occasional customer. He'd supplied the girls with drugs to keep them under his control. Though he hadn't killed Teri Riggs, everyone in the Dallas PD knew he'd killed another of his prostitutes a few years earlier, but no one had been able to make the case.

Sitting up—somehow she felt too vulnerable lying down while Decker sat a few yards away—she politely asked, "How's your mama?"

He blinked, expecting her usual self-defense, caught off-guard by the change. "She's fine."

"Still painting, papering or reupholstering everything that doesn't move?"

"Yeah." He tugged at his ear, a sign of discomfort. "She's going to do this place when I get it finished."

"I take it the outside is her work."

"Yeah. She chose the colors, had 'em remove all the curly stuff and got someone to build that porch swing."

"Your dad must be grateful to have her attention turned elsewhere."

He grunted, then somewhat grudgingly asked, "How are *your* folks?"

"They're fine, too. Mom is on a dig in Peru, and Dad and Katherine are summering in Alaska." Together, her parents were the most dysfunctional people she'd ever known. Separately, they were competent, passionate people. Too bad their passions didn't include their children.

Masiela had been seventeen when they'd divorced, and it had broken her heart. Thirty-six now, she wondered sometimes if that was why she'd never married…though her sister blamed it on the men she met in her work. Cops and criminals: neither known for making the most stable of husbands.

"And the kids?"

Five years separated her and the twins, but she had always felt more like a second mother than an older sister. "Yelina is pregnant with her third child, all girls, and lives in Austin, and Elian is in Houston. Still not thinking about settling down."

"Like you."

"I've thought about it," she disagreed. Not in terms of *I could spend the rest of my life with this guy,* but more like *my biological clock is running out.* She'd never met anyone she wanted to spend her entire life with…but that nasty honest streak forced her to admit Decker had come close.

"You're just too busy getting bad guys out of jail to do anything about it."

Again she stifled a sigh. All trains of thought led back to the same depot: his insistence on taking her career choice personally. She didn't bother to remind him that she'd never gotten involved in any of his cases. She knew him, trusted him and trusted his work. She also knew that some of his fellow detectives weren't nearly as conscientious about their investigations. Sometimes they were just sloppy. Sometimes they let themselves fixate so narrowly on one suspect that they ignored the evidence pointing elsewhere.

And sometimes they were guilty themselves and were planting evidence to lead elsewhere.

"You're not settled, either," she pointed out.

He snorted. "I'm not leaving Copper Lake. I'm not changing jobs. I bought a house, I go to the neighborhood cookouts and I'll even open the door to the pesky little trick-or-treaters who come around this Halloween. How much more settled can I get?"

"You can find a wife and have some little trick-or-treaters of your own." She said the words lightly, determined to ignore the faint twinge inside.

Something that looked suspiciously like a blush spread across his face, sharpening her twinge. In their years together, she'd seen him teased, flirted with, shamelessly propositioned and damn near seduced in public, but she had never seen him blush.

She'd been relieved, earlier, to learn that he wasn't married. But that didn't mean things couldn't change in the very near future.

Decker in love. What would that be like? He was a good date—she knew that from all the times they'd doubled. He wasn't the best-looking guy around, but there was something so damn attractive about him—that sense of honesty. Loyalty. Honor. He had confidence by the truckload, his grin was wickedly charming and his body...there was something truly wicked about *it,* too. There had never been a shortage of women wanting his attention.

But it was hard to imagine *one* woman. Hard to imagine him in love.

Hard to forget that, in the beginning, she'd been half

in love with him herself. But then she'd realized that it was likely gratitude instead, because he'd taken her on as a partner when no one else wanted her, and he'd treated her with respect.

"So who's the lucky woman?"

Before she could decide whether he intended to answer, the doorbell rang. He slid to his feet, grabbed some money from an ashtray on the counter, then went down the hall.

Voices drifted back to her, Decker's a low rumble, the other younger, less self-assured. "You ordered the doc's favorite," the delivery guy said, "but I don't see her car."

Decker said something Masiela couldn't quite make out. Her own face flushing now, she stood up from the sofa and went to the cabinets to find plates and napkins. He hadn't remembered *her* taste in pizza, but his girlfriend's. And she was a doctor, no less. A selfless do-gooder who saved people's lives, while Masiela was only a step above the scum she defended and too often sent out to prey once more on innocent victims.

It was a good thing she wasn't looking for his affection, though she did miss his friendship. How long had it taken her to stop reaching for the phone whenever she needed support or encouragement or a verbal kick in the ass? How many times had she driven halfway to his apartment before remembering that he wouldn't let her in? How often had she found herself standing outside the greasy little burger joint where they'd met for dinner every Tuesday, before she remembered he'd dumped her?

She'd had other friends outside the department, and they'd filled in nicely. But he'd been her best friend. He'd been the one she could always count on. The one she'd thought would never let her down.

The only one who ever had really let her down.

By the time he returned to the kitchen with the pizzas, she'd set a shaker of Parmesan cheese and another of hot chili peppers next to the plates and was taking a can of pop from the refrigerator for herself. "Beer, pop or water?" she asked carelessly, as if she hadn't overheard the conversation.

"Pop."

She took out a can for him, then bumped the refrigerator with her hip to close it. From opposite sides of the counter, they selected their pizza, doctored the slices, gathered napkins and pop, then went to sit at different ends of the sofa. Decker propped his feet up, balancing his plate on his lap, then picked up the remote, flipping through the channels until he found a baseball game. He kept the volume low, though.

Masiela concentrated on the pizza. The crust was wheat and perfectly thin, just strong enough to support the toppings, not one speck of flour more; and the sauce was delicious, with a hint of sweetness to offset the spice. There was a smoky flavor to the cheese, and the veggies were tender-crisp, just the way she liked them.

Without glancing her way, Decker asked, "How's it rank?"

He liked pizza—pretty much all pizza. She, on the other hand, was a connoisseur and had ranked every place she'd ever gone to accordingly. It had become such a joke between them that he'd started ranking pizza joints he went to without her. "This one's definitely at the top of the list. It's about as close to perfect as I've ever had."

"So it gets an eight?"

A star for each slice in the box—the highest score

she'd ever granted. She took another bite of mushroom, onion, yellow pepper and delicately ripe tomato and sighed. "Maybe a nine. Maybe, piping hot from the oven, a ten."

He chuckled, a sound she'd thought she would never hear again, and something shivered through her. *Exhaustion,* she told herself. She'd been living on edge for weeks now, afraid to set foot outside, afraid of another break-in, another shooting, another threat. For the first time in too long, she felt secure. Bad things might still happen when Decker was around, but there was nothing they couldn't survive together.

That was all it was. Just relief at being safe. Not bone-deep affection. Not that old partners connection they'd shared. Not the faintest hope that they could share anything again, even the most casual of friendships.

She was here to keep herself safe, not to set herself up for another major disappointment at Decker's hands. He'd let her down once, and it had hurt—*God,* more than anything she'd ever been through. She wouldn't let it happen again.

It was after nine when AJ finished work in the living and dining rooms. He unplugged the tools, then stood for a moment, looking at all he'd done. He'd been in the house since the beginning of the year, and it seemed he was going to be living in a construction zone a whole lot longer. In the beginning, he'd felt a real sense of accomplishment when he'd managed to do something by himself—and do it right. Now it was just one more job to check off on a list that was endless.

He should check off a lot of jobs in the next week.

He switched off the lights, then went into the kitchen. The television was on, but Masiela wasn't watching it.

She'd leaned onto the sofa arm, her own arms under her head, and was sleeping, head at an awkward angle, feet tucked up beside her.

After taking a bottle of water from the refrigerator, he shut off the light over the sink, then went to stand in front of her.

"Hey."

She didn't stir.

"Masiela."

No response.

Grimacing, he laid his hand on her shoulder. "Hey, Mas. Get up and I'll help you fold out the couch."

He gave her a shake and she jerked upright, her right hand whipping down to her waist, unholstering her pistol in one smooth move. Even while he admired her quick reflexes after so many years off the job, he stepped back, his hand raised palm out. "Whoa, whoa, Mas, come on. You shoot me in my own house, you're gonna have to call the police and the ambulance, and people are gonna know you're here, and Donovan's gonna be really pissed."

She stared at him, her expression stark, her eyes dazed for the moment it took her to come fully awake. She blinked, then lowered the gun. "Jesus, AJ. Don't do that."

AJ. She'd called him that when they'd first met—when he had volunteered to partner with her—but she'd decided within a day or so that it didn't feel right. After that, like everyone else in the department, she'd called him by his last name. Except for that one night.

He backed off, and she set the gun on the end table, then shoved her hair back from her face. "Sorry."

"Yeah. I'm going upstairs. You want help with the couch?"

"Sure." She stood, stretching out a kink, pulling her T-shirt above the waistband of her jeans, displaying an inch or two of smooth, brown skin.

It was just a strip of her stomach. He saw more exposed skin every day in warm weather, on the joggers, the kids hanging out at the community pool, the young women shopping downtown. Hell, he'd seen more of *her* skin plenty of times—all the hours in the gym, all the time spent together off duty…that night, when he'd seen it all.

He forced his gaze away, forced himself to move back, to lift the coffee table and carry it to the side, near the kitchen counter. When he turned back, she had removed the seat cushions and stacked them on the table, then, together, they pulled the bed frame from the couch. It came with a creak, never-before-moved metal complaining as it shifted into new positions. The thin mattress unfolded with a flop, looking about as comfortable as the bare wood floor in the living room.

"Thanks," Masiela said, as she shook out a sheet so the fabric floated down across the flowered ticking. "I can take it from here."

He was happy to leave her to it. As he walked down the hall, he opened the bathroom door, switched on the light, then left the door partway open. He didn't want her stumbling around in the dark, looking for the bathroom, not when he was even faster with a gun than she was.

In the safety of his room, he showered and shaved, then settled in bed with the bottled water and the TV on. He was still vaguely sore from Willie's kick—and acutely aware that his privacy had been violated. No one had ever spent the night there but Cate, and that was at his invitation. No one even visited besides Cate, unless it was to help on some project—again, at his invitation.

He could have told Donovan no. Should have.

But if he had, and Masiela had returned to Texas and something had happened to her... Of all the people he knew, she was the very last one he wanted on his conscience.

The phone on the bedside table rang, with a faint echo from downstairs. He grabbed it before the ring silenced, not that he cared if it woke Masiela, but because he didn't want her forgetting and picking it up. Though reason made him admit that what she'd said earlier was true: she wasn't stupid. She wouldn't do anything to endanger herself.

It was Cate. He'd known it would be. If it were police business, the call would come in on his cell phone, and anyone else would wait until morning. Only Cate made a habit of calling him around bedtime on nights when she worked.

"I miss you," she said, in place of a greeting.

"Yeah." The best he could offer. He'd thought about her a time or two this evening, but not in the wish-she-was-here sort of way. More of a hope that she didn't find out about Mas, and an oh yeah, Cate likes veggie pizza too realization.

"I've come to the conclusion that you're one of the few men in this town who has developed beyond the moron stage."

"I'm gonna guess you've had an E.R. full of stupid guys doing stupid things tonight."

"Car surfing, skateboarding with a towrope tied to the bumper of a car, contests to see who can hold a lighted firecracker the longest.... Sheesh, if women didn't need men to procreate, we'd let them kill themselves off."

He snorted. "Most of you are more interested in recreating than procreating."

"I certainly am. Especially with you." The soft, sexy tone switched to matter-of-fact. "Too bad I'm stuck here in the hospital for the next God knows how many hours. My relief—a man—is going to be late *again*."

"Yeah, too bad," he echoed, more because it seemed appropriate than because of any genuine desire. He was sore, Masiela was downstairs, and he was suddenly feeling…odd. Suspiciously like something that might have slithered out from under a rock.

"I heard about your run-in with Willie." Cate's voice was light with amusement. "Unless the details were greatly exaggerated, it's probably a good thing that I'll be on duty most of the night."

He scowled. His testicles had probably been the subject of gossip in more places than the hospital. Wasn't that nice to know? "If the details included me curled up on the ground, barely able to breathe, they're not exaggerated."

"Poor baby. You'll be fine in a day or two." Another voice filtered over the phone, then she said, "Sorry, I've got to go. Got a patient in. Talk to you tomorrow?"

"Sure." He hung up, shut off the lamp, then gazed at the shadows from the television flickering on the wall. He'd said enough to Masiela that she'd guessed he was thinking about getting married, and he was. It just seemed like maybe it was time, and he'd been seeing Cate for nearly a year. She was long over her divorce, and had hinted that she was ready to give marriage another shot. They got along great, they'd never fought, they had plenty in common—he liked her a lot. Why not get married? They'd be good together.

As long as she wasn't expecting something like, oh, a husband who loved her. Because he did like her very much, but he didn't love her. She wasn't the most important person in his life. If she wasn't around, he would miss her for a while, but his life wasn't going to fall apart because she wasn't in it.

Getting along, liking, not fighting…were those good enough reasons to get married?

Maybe for him. Probably not for Cate.

Did she think he felt the feelings but just hadn't said the words? Had he led her on by not saying anything at all? By not running the other way when she mentioned marriage?

Too complicated a line of thought when he was feeling tired and sore and a bit reptilian. He settled more comfortably in bed, inhaled deeply, catching a faint whiff of Cate's perfume on the pillows, then exhaled deeply and drifted to sleep.

Morning came too soon, the steady *beep-beep* of the alarm clock making his teeth grind before he punched the button that stopped the noise. He threw back the covers and sat up, and a dull discomfort reminded him of yesterday's fun.

Fuzzy-headed, he brushed his teeth, then splashed water onto his face to help him wake up. He normally got up feeling pretty rested and alert, but normally didn't include a knee to the groin, weird dreams…and a blast from the past.

Dressed in jeans and a yellow polo shirt embroidered with the CLPD logo and his name, AJ went downstairs. The bathroom door was still open, the light still on. He cut through the living and dining rooms to the kitchen—not necessarily avoiding Masiela, but rather the narrow squeeze between the foot of the bed and the TV—and switched on the light over the sink. The coffeemaker stood nearby, a travel mug already in place.

Quickly, quietly, he measured coffee grounds into one compartment, filtered water into another, pressed the Start button, then waited impatiently.

The sky was starting to lighten behind the house. Out front, the eastern horizon would be changing colors as the sun rose. The air would be warm, but not uncomfortably so. That would start around nine, with the temperature rising and the humidity climbing with it. By two it would be damn hot and muggy, and he would be wondering why, if he'd had to relocate from Dallas, he hadn't gone north. Someplace along the Canadian border—or, hell, even Alaska sounded better than Georgia in June.

Except he'd rather sweat in a steambath every summer than face snow, ice or subzero temperatures in the winter.

The coffeemaker gurgled to a stop, and he pulled the cup away. He'd stirred in sweetener and two tiny tubs of cream and was about to take the first sip when a wide-awake voice came from across the room.

"Still can't start your day without coffee, huh?"

AJ looked at the couch for the first time and saw Masiela lying on her side, the pillow folded in half beneath her head, the sheet tucked under her arms. She looked soft and mussed and incredibly beautiful. He'd thought that the first time he'd seen her—that she was incredibly beautiful, and that it was a good thing he wasn't affected by incredible beauty, since it might interfere with his teaching her the new job.

He still wasn't affected by beauty. He *wasn't*. He was just staring because having someone else in his house was keeping him unbalanced.

Quietly he snorted. Yep, Masiela had done a good job of keeping him unbalanced over the years.

"Doesn't smell like your usual Jamaica Blue Mountain." She sat up, letting the sheet fall to her waist, and turned to lean against the sofa arm, knees drawn to her chest. She was wearing a tank top, black, ribbed, molding to her breasts.

What was under the sheet? He couldn't help but wonder. Shorts? Tiny panties? Matching, of course. She'd always had a thing for matching lingerie, the skimpier, the better.

Swallowing hard, he took that first sip, dark and mildly acidic, then remembered her comment. He shook his head, not sure his voice would work, but tried it anyway. "It's not. It's a Salvadoran blend. Ayutepeque. The guy who owns the coffee shop in town gets it for me. You want a cup?"

She looked tempted but shook her head. "I've been jumpy enough the past few weeks. I don't need any extra caffeine."

"There's not much here in the way of food," he began, but she waved one hand.

"I've got leftover pizza. That'll cover breakfast and lunch."

"Make up a shopping list and I'll pick up groceries after work. You do still cook, don't you?"

"I do. You do still eat anything anyone sets in front of you, don't you?"

"Yeah."

Cate joked about it. She was so lousy a cook that even her dog wouldn't eat her efforts—but AJ did.

Thinking about Cate while looking at Masiela—or avoiding looking at her—stirred a twinge of guilt. He snapped a lid on the travel mug, then scooped up his keys from the counter. "I've got to go. If you need anything—"

"I'll just dial 911."

Though he knew she was teasing, he scowled anyway. "My cell phone number's taped inside the cabinet door." His mother could keep track of a hundred different paint samples and fabric swatches, but she lost phone numbers the way a dog shed hair.

Masiela gave him a halfhearted salute, then moved as if to push back the covers—his cue to get out. Fast.

Chapter 3

It was amazing how quiet an old house could be. If not for the noises Masiela was making—folding bedding, manhandling the bed frame back into the sofa—there would be utter silence. Not a board creaking, not a whisper from the central air or a hum from the refrigerator. In her condo, she always heard something: the normal sounds of the house, her neighbors fighting or making love, their kids playing, traffic moving through the complex.

Lifting her suitcase onto the sofa, she unpacked toiletries and a clean set of clothes, picked up her pistol, shoved her feet into a pair of flip-flops and headed upstairs for a shower.

Four doors lined the hallway, only one of them open. She set her things on the bathroom counter, then went back to the hall. The first door opened into a bedroom stacked haphazardly with furniture and unmarked boxes. So did the second. It was like Decker not to label anything…though it was also like him to have a pretty good idea of what was where without labels.

The last door led to his room. She hesitated, fingers wrapped around the knob. This was his private space, and a closed door definitely didn't constitute an invitation to enter.

But he'd told her to make herself at home. And what if something happened while he was gone? Wasn't it in her best interests to be totally familiar with her environment?

Weak excuse, she chided herself as she opened the door anyway and stepped inside.

At his last apartment in Dallas, his bedroom had had dirty white walls, mismatched furniture and a badly worn carpet that was rarely seen, thanks to the clothing and detritus scattered over it all the time. The place looked as if it belonged to a college kid with zero budget, she'd teased him, but he hadn't cared.

That was the difference. In Dallas he hadn't given a damn what his bedroom looked like. Now he did.

The walls were painted buff, and the furniture actually matched. The bed was made, though she would have bet he didn't know how to make a bed. A primitive-looking piece in the corner hid a clothes hamper underneath its lift-up lid, and a plain sturdy chair occupied the opposite corner. There were even pictures on the walls.

It was a lovely room. The college kid with zero budget and less taste had grown into a man with serious taste.

Unless, she thought with a grin, his mother was responsible for all this.

Or—and the grin disappeared—his girlfriend.

She showered and dressed, then brushed her teeth. It felt funny, propping her toothbrush in the holder beside his, leaving her hair products and shaving cream and razor next to his. It felt intimate, which they weren't. Would never again be.

Clipping the gun holster onto the waistband of her shorts, Masiela returned to the kitchen. After eating two pieces of cold pizza and drinking a bottle of water at the counter, she looked around.

She'd showered and eaten breakfast. Making up the sofa bed had taken care of the housework. Now she had nothing to do but read or watch TV and wait for Decker to return home. She'd never had an entire week with nothing to do...or an entire week where she couldn't set so much as one foot outside the door. She might die of boredom.

There wasn't much of the house left to explore. She walked into the dusty room across from the living room, crossed the hall and circled through the dining room and back into the kitchen, before checking out the room next to the bathroom, which appeared to be a library. The only room left was next door, a decent-size laundry room that held a washer and dryer, along with most of the things that would be stored in a garage.

Stepping around bottles of motor oil and bleach, she went to the door opposite the washer. The top half was glass, partially covered by a curtain on a glass rod, and the bottom was wood. Through the window, she could see pale peach walls on both sides.

Hesitantly she rested her fingers on the lock. In the back of her mind, an annoying voice—Decker's, of course—was repeating his order that she stay inside and out of sight, but still her fingers tightened, then twisted the lock. She opened the door just enough to peek out and saw three steps that led to a tiny recessed stoop, neatly blocked from view on both sides by the house.

The only way anyone could possibly see her there was to hide in the woods at the edge of the yard, and if someone was out there spying on her, they could see her just as easily through the windows in the kitchen and dining room. As she stepped out, the breeze was pleasantly cool on her skin and helped clear the smells of remodeling from her lungs.

What AJ didn't know wouldn't hurt him, she decided as she eased to the floor, knees drawn up, ankles crossed. The wood beneath her was painted deep green, playing off the peach walls and the cream steps. She'd never met Mrs. Decker, but she'd have to give her credit for two things: great taste and raising a good, if hardheaded, son. He could be a little more reasonable, but granted, couldn't most men?

As the wind picked up, Masiela rested her head against the wall and wondered what was going on in Dallas. Had Donovan spoken to his boss yet? Did Kinney and his pals have any idea how close they were to being in handcuffs themselves?

What if Donovan, or his boss, chose to do nothing? The state didn't like it when news broke that they'd given an innocent man a life sentence, and politics being as dirty as they were, they could decide on a cover-up instead of an exposé. She would still have options. It was just that having the cooperation of the DA's office would make the whole process easier.

She wished she could talk to Donovan, but he'd be livid if she called and rightly so. Just as Decker would be pissed if he knew she'd set foot outside. He had no patience for too-stupid-to-live people.

With one last breath of sweetly scented air, Masiela stood up, then froze as a dog bounded out of the tree line seventy-five feet away. A short distance behind him came a teenage boy, his attention locked on the cell phone in his hands. He was texting, which caused him to stumble over an exposed tree root. With the self-consciousness inborn in teenage boys, he glanced around to see if anyone had noticed, and she pressed herself flat against the house.

If his gaze touched her, she couldn't say. He gave no indication, but merely shook his hair back from his face, returned to texting and followed the dog toward the back of the house next door.

He disappeared from her view, and she counted to ten, then darted inside and locked the door. For good measure, she whipped the curtains shut. That was too close. Granted, he was just a kid, thirteen, maybe fourteen years old. But it could have been anyone—even, if they'd managed to track her to Georgia, one of the Brat Pack.

Hating the furtive feeling between her shoulder blades, she located a few items in the linen closet upstairs, along with a hammer and nails in the living room. With a silent promise to replace the sheet, she hammered nails along the top edge, forming a curtain over the dining room window. On the smaller window over the sink, she made do with a couple of pillowcases, blocking the view and making her feel slightly better hidden.

The word made her cross. Here she was, hiding like a coward, while the men responsible were free to go where they chose, wearing their badges, carrying their guns, abusing their authority. "What's wrong with *that* picture?" she muttered.

Nothing that she couldn't change.

If she lived long enough.

"Your friend didn't stick around long."

AJ looked up from the lab reports spread across his

desk as Tommy Maricci slid into the chair, picked up a manila folder and began flipping through it. "My—oh. Donovan. Nah, he was just passing through. Just stopped to say hello."

"He a good prosecutor?"

"One of the best."

"Maybe you could persuade him to move here. The verdict just came in on the Terrell case. The jury let him off."

"Damn." Steve Terrell was a punk, a small time loser drug dealer. The only way a jury could have acquitted him was if Benton Tatum, the DA, had phoned in his arguments from his riverside fishing hole. It seemed he'd been doing a lot of that lately.

"Donovan's got bigger plans than Copper Lake can afford. He's got integrity, an excellent conviction rate and family money. I figure he's gonna be attorney general someday." No matter how Masiela's so-called case turned out. If she persuaded Donovan that he had prosecuted the wrong man, instead of having a black mark against him, Donovan would set things right in a way that would strengthen his reputation.

Depending on your definition of "right." Three good cops would be destroyed. A murderer would go free. The distrust that already existed between the police and some segments of the population they protected would intensify.

But Masiela would be satisfied that she'd won, and for her, that was enough to justify anything.

A twinge of something niggled in his gut. Guilt? Wrongheadedness? Was he carrying loyalty too far by refusing to even listen to her so-called evidence?

His first answer was no. He knew the officers in question, had known them a hell of a lot longer than he'd known Masiela. And he'd watched her in court, twisting things the witnesses said, implying deceit when there was none, using words to create doubt that didn't exist. She'd excused it as simply doing her job.

He couldn't excuse it.

"How's it going at the house?" Maricci asked.

He thought first of his unwanted guest, then realized Maricci was referring to the work. "I've done as much as I can on the living and dining rooms, until I get an extra set of hands."

"I can come over this evening. Ellie and Anamaria are taking a class at Sophy's shop tonight. They're learning to make baby quilts."

Surprise stifled the automatic refusal AJ was about to give. "Really?" When Maricci had broken up with Ellie last year, he'd begun seeing Sophy Marchand, only to leave her to go back to Ellie when she became the prime suspect in a murder investigation.

Maricci's grin was sheepish. "Sophy doesn't hold a grudge."

"Nah, she's got Isaacs to do that for her." For a day or two, Kiki Isaacs had been the detective handling that investigation. As Sophy's best friend, she'd taken great pleasure in harassing Ellie.

"After dinner?" Maricci asked, referring to his offer.

"Uh…tonight's not good. Let me get back to you."

"Sure. Speaking of Isaacs…" Maricci shifted in the chair. "She's driving Ty nuts. Reminding him every hour that she's superior to him, giving him orders and generally making things tough for him. Talk to her, would you?"

AJ scowled. Ty Gadney was the department's newest detective; Isaacs had been on the job a whole nine months. She was a good cop, but she was a huge pain in everyone's ass, especially his. Ambitious, eager to prove herself in an all-male division, she was like a rampaging bull, charging over anyone who got in her way. Her ego apparently put Gadney in her sights more often than not.

Maricci closed the file, a report of crime statistics for the first half of the year, and put it back in its place on the desk. "I thought I'd take Ty with me to interview the hit-and-run from yesterday morning and leave Kiki to you."

"Thanks," AJ said drily as Maricci left the office. He'd rather face anyone today than Kiki. Except Masiela. Maybe. At least she didn't make him crazy the way Kiki did.

But the only danger he was in with Kiki was of a legal nature, if he lost control and wrapped his hands tightly around her throat; while Masiela...

She'd screwed with him in a way no one ever had. He'd cared too much about her and lost too much when she'd left. He wasn't about to let that happen again. Damn Ray Donovan. He'd have been happier to pretend she never existed.

Maricci hadn't been gone ten minutes when Kiki came into his office. She wore the same jeans and yellow polo shirt the other detectives did; it just looked appreciably different on her. Her brown hair, prone to frizzing wildly in the humidity, was pulled back tightly and contained in a braid, and her face was settled in a pout. Not unusual for the woman referred to as the department's biggest whiner.

More than a few of her fellow officers thought she'd been promoted to detective only because she was a woman—something Masiela knew about. In Masiela's case, it wasn't true, but AJ couldn't deny that had been part of his reason for selecting Kiki. The chief had instructed him to promote a woman, and she'd been the best-qualified of the handful in the department.

She plopped into the chair and folded her arms over her chest. "Tommy took Ty with him and left *me* here to write reports on this morning's calls."

"When you're as senior as he is, you get to do that," AJ said mildly. "Besides, you write better reports than he does. At least you spell everything right."

"It's because I'm a *girl,* and everyone knows girls are better suited to jobs like typing and writing."

"I partnered with a woman in Dallas, and I was way better at that stuff than she was." Damn, he just couldn't seem to get Masiela out of his mind. Understandable maybe, since she was in his house. Still, he'd like to forget that, at least while he was out of the house himself.

"He told me to do my nails."

That sounded like Maricci.

"He picks on me because I'm a girl."

Woman, AJ mentally corrected. "You know, you did try to make a homicide case against his wife," he reminded her. Maricci wasn't an expert at holding grudges like Kiki, but that would be a little hard to overlook.

"She wasn't his wife at the time, and the evidence—"

"Was manufactured." It had been designed to make a so-so cop focus on Ellie and no one else, and that was what Kiki, in her inexperience, had done. Lucky for Ellie, Tommy had been on her side. Luckier still that Kiki's father had had a mild heart attack and AJ had taken over the investigation himself while she stayed with him during his recovery.

Kiki brushed it off with a shrug. Ellie had never been

arrested, so in Kiki's opinion, no harm, no foul. It wasn't an attitude AJ liked to see in his people.

"I don't see why I couldn't have gone out with Ty to interview the hit-and-run victim."

"Because Detective Maricci asked you to stay here." *Told* was probably more accurate, but AJ tried to be diplomatic...to a point. "I know you've been in the detective division for nine months, Kiki, but that's still pretty new. You still have to do what you're told. You don't get to make a lot of decisions, and you don't get to train anyone else."

Her gaze narrowed. "Did Ty complain to you?"

"Haven't heard a word from him." He was glad he could say it with total honesty.

Her gaze narrowed even more, and her lower lip poked out. "Tommy?"

"Even when I'm not around, Isaacs, I keep track of what's going on in my division." When she started to speak, he raised one hand to stop her. "One of these days, Kiki, you'll be the senior detective—hell, maybe the lieutenant. Then you'll have all the control you want. But you've got to earn it. Until then, do your job the best you can and try to be a team player. Don't complain so much. Everyone in this office has to do jobs they don't like until they get senior enough to palm them off on someone else. Suck it up and move on."

She sat there a moment, still pouting, then grudgingly got to her feet. "So I continue getting stuck in the office doing the girly jobs."

AJ's voice was strained. "Doing the jobs you're told to do."

"Yeah, the girly stuff," she repeated. "Because, hey, I'm a girl."

With an exaggerated sense of martyrdom, Kiki left

the office, disquiet in the air in her wake. AJ rubbed his eyes as he forced his jaw to relax.

"She didn't hear a single thing you said."

He looked up, his gaze connecting with Cate's as she stepped into the open doorway. That feeling from last night—the crawled-from-under-a-rock one—reappeared as she closed the door, then leaned against it and smiled at him. "Hey."

"Hey."

She was pretty in a wholesome, middle-America, girl-next-door way: short brown hair, blue eyes, easy smile. She reached five-four only if she stretched, she favored jeans and T-shirts when she wasn't wearing scrubs, she never put any pressure on him and she was sweet. Never moody, never difficult, never taking sides he couldn't agree with. She was pretty much perfect.

Except for that damn love thing.

"Kiki will grow up sometime," Cate said optimistically, as she started across the room. "She'll turn your hair gray first, but it'll happen."

"You promise?"

She circled his desk, her movements purposeful. He liked purposeful. He didn't need fluid or naturally graceful or inherently sensual, didn't need to be distracted from what she was doing by the way she was doing it. Like Masiela, when she clipped her weapon onto her waistband. Or when she'd shoved her hair back from her face last night. Or when she'd tasted the first bite of Luigi's pizza.

Damn it. He'd worked hard over the years to avoid thinking about her, and now he couldn't keep her out of his mind, not even with Cate slowly approaching.

Scowling, he focused hard on Cate instead. "What are you doing out this morning?"

She smiled as brightly as if she hadn't worked through the middle of the night. "I got hungry, so I thought maybe you could join me for lunch."

It wasn't unusual. They did it every week or two—sometimes at his house. Sandwiches in bed. *That* was out for the time being: his house, his bed, her bed. It wouldn't feel right.

Nothing felt right at the moment.

"I appreciate the offer," he said, turning in his chair as she finally reached him. She leaned against the edge of the desk, her knee between his, and held out her hand for his. He let her take it, let her twine her fingers with his. It was a familiar gesture. Comfortable. But about as intimate as holding hands with his sister.

"But?" Cate prompted.

"I, uh, I've got some things to take care of at lunch." It was a lie when he said it, but as soon as the words were out, he realized the truth. He needed to go by the house and make sure everything was okay. He might not want Masiela there, but since she was, damned if anything was going to happen to her on his watch. And he really should take her some food. Yeah, she'd said leftover pizza would be fine for lunch, but even *she* had limits on how much pizza she could eat.

"Okay," Cate said. Nothing changed—not her smile, her tone, her mood. She didn't care that he'd turned down her invitation. Shouldn't it have mattered?

Maybe she wasn't so much in love as comfortable with him.

He should be affronted, but all he felt was a vague sense of relief.

"I think I'll head over to Ellie's Deli then." Standing, she leaned forward to brush a kiss to his cheek. "I'll call you."

"Be careful."

She flashed him a brighter smile as she opened the door. "What's the fun in that?"

By noon, Masiela's edginess had given way to boredom, defined in two easy words: daytime television. Cooking shows, talk shows, game shows, soap operas, decorating shows… She was in hell, and she hadn't even died yet.

She was standing in the dining room, gazing out the window—truthfully, peeking out like a coward—at the yard that needed mowing and maybe a picket fence and definitely some flowers, when the phone rang. The sound startled her, and instinctively she took a step toward it before remembering that she wasn't supposed to answer.

After the third ring, the answering machine clicked on, and a moment later came Decker's voice. "I'm in the driveway. Don't shoot me when I come in."

She smiled thinly. There were times when shooting him held a certain appeal, but then there would be that mess to clean up. And how would she explain it to his parents and Donovan?

By the time he came into the kitchen, she was standing at the dining peninsula, a half-empty bottle of water in front of her. He carried a couple of plastic grocery bags in one hand, a paper bag bearing a fast-food logo in the other.

His grin could be charming, his smile polished, but the scowl he wore now looked most at home on his features. He was the kind of guy who could intimidate people with nothing more than that. She, being smaller, thinner and a woman, had had to rely on other means of intimidation—a pistol, pepper spray, tough talk accompanied by tougher follow-through, in the guise of a bone-jarring control hold.

"I thought you might want something besides pizza." He set the paper bag between them, sliding it toward her, and the fragrance of fried beef and onions drifted into the air. It was enough to make her mouth water, and the sight of her favorite cookies as he began unloading the grocery bags finished the job.

He glanced at the dining room window, then the kitchen window. His eyes were expressionless, his tone mild, when he asked, "You worried about too much sun in here?"

Masiela tried to sound as mild. "There was a kid out back this morning. Came out of the woods and across the yard to the house next door. It just made me realize that hiding isn't really hiding when anyone who happens by can see me." The odds that someone would track her from Dallas to Copper Lake were slim, but stranger things had happened. Though there was no substitute for good detective work, there was also no substitute for luck. Citizens might feel less safe if they knew how often luck played a role in solving crimes.

"Skinny kid, needs a haircut, texting someone?"

She nodded.

"That's Speed. He and his sister live with their aunt Pris next door. Mom's in jail, Dad doesn't want them, so they wound up here. The girl, Calie, is a little mouse. I figure I'll be arresting Speed before too long. He's pissed off at the world and showing it."

"What's the nickname for? His drug of choice? His driving?"

AJ shook his head. "Apparently, he was one hell of a runner before he came here. He's only thirteen, but did half marathons, won lots of races. According to his aunt, pretty much all he does here is hang out alone in the woods and text his best friend back home."

"Someone should probably get the kid back into running. You know, someone who lives nearby, who could be a positive male influence in his life."

AJ scowled. "I'm a cop, not a social worker."

"Sometimes the line between the two gets blurry." She'd heard the words from him first. They'd been interviewing witnesses in a case and had come across a man whose wife had left him and their kids in a seedy apartment not fit for cockroaches. She'd been all set to call social services to take the kids, but AJ had intervened. *Clean the place up,* he'd told the man. *We'll be back in two hours to check.*

In those two hours, they'd gone grocery shopping, picking up enough food, formula and diapers to get the family through the next few weeks, and he'd continued to check up on them until the man's relatives had come through with their own help.

"I think Speed needs more than a running partner."

"Of course he does. He needs a father." She shrugged. "But you make do with what you have."

He didn't pursue that statement—he could hardly argue when he knew she spoke from experience, could he?—and wadded the plastic bags. She gazed at the items he'd bought: cookies, BBQ potato chips, chocolate, bags of cherries and grapes, a box of tea bags and another of sweetener packets. Every one her favorites. She'd thought last night that he'd ordered his girlfriend's favorite pizza by mistake, though it was coincidentally her favorite, too. But all this couldn't be a coincidence.

He'd remembered.

He stuffed the bags in a drawer, then took two plates from the cabinet. "You gonna open that bag?"

"Yeah. Sure." She unfolded the top flap, and the aromas grew stronger. Inside were two burgers wrapped in grease-stained paper and two bags of fries. The fries were crispy and salty, the way they should be, and she popped a couple into her mouth while dividing the food between the plates.

"Do you normally come home for lunch?" She hooked a stool with her foot and pulled it over to sit on as he set two cans of pop and a bottle of ketchup on the counter.

"No."

"Will people think it's odd?"

"I don't think anyone pays that much attention to where I eat." He sat on a stool on the other side of the counter and squirted a puddle of ketchup on his plate. "Did you make a shopping list?"

She gestured toward the paper at the end of the counter. "Won't they think *that's* odd?" A man who obviously didn't cook, buying pork and chicken and pasta and veggies?

"When Mom runs out of decorating projects, she comes over sometimes and cooks. Anything that can be frozen and reheated. They'd think I was shopping for her."

"I wish my mom had done that while I was working and going to school. I had to get by with frozen diet dinners."

"Like you ever needed to watch your weight," he mumbled around a mouthful of food.

It was a nothing little compliment, way too insignificant to justify the pleasure she felt. "I'll have to after this week. Pizza, greasy burgers, Oreos and no exercise. I can already feel my butt expanding."

He made a noise that sounded like a disbelieving snort, and that way overblown pleasure warmed. It felt almost like old times…though that *almost* was an awfully big one. There was too much between them for things to ever be the way they used to. She needed to remember that. Besides, the way they used to be wasn't what she'd really wanted. She'd settled for friendship because it was all he'd offered, except for that one night.

They'd never spoken of it. Never. The next morning he was gone when she awakened, and when she'd dragged herself into work with one hellacious hangover, he acted as if nothing had happened. She'd waited all shift for him to say something, but he didn't. Not one word, one action, not even one look hinting that he'd seen her naked. *She* was the one who'd gotten drunk, yet *he'd* developed blackout amnesia.

And since he never mentioned it, neither had she—and eight years later seemed a hell of a time to bring it up, especially considering all that had gone wrong between them.

"Everything okay around here besides Speed?" he asked between bites.

She nodded. "No phone calls, no deliveries, no prowlers, no door-to-door salesmen."

"We don't have those in Copper Lake. Though there are the occasional church people who go out inviting folks to Sunday school."

He fished a pickle off his burger and dropped it on the rim of his plate. Without thinking, she picked it up and popped it into her mouth, savoring the crunch of pickle, the tang of mustard and the flavor of the beef patty it had nestled against. When Decker gave her a narrowed look, she realized what she'd done and winced inside. New relationship, new circumstances. So what if she'd always eaten the pickles off his burgers? That was then, and now was different.

"I might welcome a visit from a hellfire-and-brimstone believer," she said. "At least it would be a break from the monotony of the TV."

"If you wanted excitement, you should have stayed in Dallas."

She gave him a sarcastic smile before taking the last bite of her burger. After washing it down with a drink of pop, she wiped her hands and mouth on a napkin, then wadded it. "I'm not looking for excitement. Just something to do."

"Like what?"

She glanced around. Getting outside to work in his yard, no matter how badly it needed her touch, was out of the question, and obviously, so was a trip to a nursery for flowers. There wasn't any real cleaning to do, no dishes to wash, no laundry overflowing the hampers. "I don't know. I could...help out."

"With what?"

"I don't know," she repeated, then her gaze fell on the doorway barely visible in the hall. "I assume your plans for that room don't include painting the wood. I could strip it."

The offer surprised her almost as much as him. Of all the rooms, the library had the biggest potential, with its tall shelves and elaborate window and door casings and black marble fireplace. The wallpaper was ancient, dark flowers on a darker background, and the drapes at the windows were burgundy and suffocating, but when all that was gone and the wood had received a new finish, it would be a lovely, cozy room.

Decker blinked, then took their plates to the sink and tossed the wrappers into the trash before he faced her again. "Have you ever stripped hundred-year-old varnish?"

"No. Have you?"

His mouth twitched as if he were almost tempted to smile, but of course, he didn't. "No. But you don't see me volunteering to do it, either. I actually had thought about painting everything in there except the fireplace."

"All that gorgeous wood? I think that would be illegal."

"That's what Russ Calloway said. Well, that it would be a crime. He's a builder who's been giving me advice. His family used to be in logging around here. Now they're in everything else. All the wood for this house came from Calloway trees."

"Nice to know the history of a place. My condo has no history. Before it was condos, it was pasture." They were personality-free, unit after identical unit. She'd been happy with it, but it was an investment more than a home. Someday, she fully intended to get married, sell the condo and have a real house to raise her kids in. A house like this.

But someday hadn't arrived quite on the schedule she'd imagined. She'd turned thirty-six on her last birthday and was no closer to marriage and kids than she'd been when she'd bought the condo.

"So?" she prompted.

He shrugged. "Yeah, sure. I'll pick up the stuff before I go to the grocery store." He glanced at his watch, then headed for the door. "I usually get off between four and five. I'll call when I get home."

Masiela let him get as far as the doorway before responding. "I'd never shoot without seeing exactly who I'm shooting."

He glanced back. "I know. I'll call."

It felt good to smile, easing some of the tension that had taken up permanent residence in her jaw and her neck. She waited until the front door closed, then went looking for a pitcher in the cabinets. The first cabinet she opened held plates and bowls, and the cell phone number he'd mentioned that morning was taped to the inside of the door. She studied it, committing it to memory, then scanned the other business cards there: Luigi's Pizza, Russ Calloway, a plumber, an electrician, a carpenter... and an emergency room doctor.

Cate Calloway. Not just a doctor, but part of the family that was into everything around Copper Lake. She was probably beautiful and delicate. Probably a blonde. Decker had always had a weakness for blondes. She probably oozed old money and good breeding and had never once felt out of place in her kingdom.

Unlike the half-Mexican, half-Cuban Leals, who'd spoken fluent Spanish before they'd picked up their first words of English, even though they'd been born in Texas. Who'd fit into their mostly Latino neighborhoods and schools, but when they ventured outside that comfort zone, had been taunted more than a few times to go back to whatever poor Latin country they'd come from.

Masiela would bet no one had ever dared tell Dr. Cate Calloway to go back to where she'd come from.

She was still scowling when she found a plastic pitcher in the cabinet beside the sink. She dropped in two tea bags, filled it with water and set it aside to steep, then breathed deeply.

Decker's taste in women was none of her concern. If he'd fallen in love with a Southern belle princess do-gooder doctor, great. She wished them all the happiness in the world. Really. And she'd do it with a sincere smile while forcing the lie between her teeth.

In the meantime... She went into the library, stopping in the middle of the room and turning in a slow circle.

The built-in shelves covered most of three walls, and the elaborately trimmed windows filled the fourth. The shelves weren't the adjustable kind, either, where she could take them out and work on them in a more convenient position. Nope. They were nailed in place, which meant she would be twisting and bending like a contortionist to do the job.

And when it was finished, when she was gone and Decker and the princess doctor got married, this would probably be the doc's home office. Her medical texts would fill Masiela's beautifully redone shelves. The lovely old chandelier overhead would shine down on her desk. She and Decker would spend cozy evenings in here before retiring to the cozier bedroom upstairs.

Masiela huffed in disgust as she went to find the ShopVac she'd seen in the living room, then began cleaning.

Chapter 4

In a better mood than he should have been, Decker parked in the police department lot and was approaching the door when it swung open and a familiar figure walked out. She saw him, and for a moment it seemed she couldn't decide whether to be amused or abashed. She settled on a combination of the two.

"Officer Decker."

"Ma'am."

This time Willie tried for a smile. It was crooked and showed nicotine-stained teeth, one missing. "How are you feeling today?"

"Like I got kicked in the nads yesterday. Have you been released?"

"For good behavior," she said, her gray head bobbing to emphasize the words.

"Miz Franklin, I doubt you have even a passing familiarity with the concept of good behavior. Do you need a ride home?"

Her gaze shifted past him while she considered it. AJ knew home for her was on the north side of Copper Lake, at least a mile-and-a-half walk in the muggy heat. It could be broken up into manageable segments, though, by stops at the bars along the way.

Finally she looked back. "Don't suppose we could run by the liquor store first."

It wasn't his place to judge her or try to force her to change. Still, he shook his head. "No, ma'am, I don't suppose so."

"Then I think I'll walk and enjoy the beautiful day." She smiled broadly and waved as she set off for the street.

He was reaching for the door when she stopped at the curb and yelled back. "Officer Decker, sorry about kicking you in the privates. I'll try not to do it again."

Chuckling came from behind him, and he scowled at two young uniformed officers coming in off patrol. They immediately wiped the humor from their faces, said polite greetings, then began snickering again once they'd gone inside.

The joys of a small town. Decker had known the move from Dallas to Copper Lake would mean some adjustments. He would miss the restaurants, sports, entertainment and all-night everything the city had to offer. He'd known there would be less privacy. It was easier to be anonymous in a city of a million-plus than one of twenty thousand.

But it really hadn't been a difficult transition. After all, he'd grown up in a town not much bigger than Copper Lake. He was used to neighbors both friendly and nosy. He didn't mind people taking more of an interest in the details of his life.

Except that there should always be something private about a man's *privates*.

He went inside, checking in at the desk on the way, and then to his office. There, he closed the door and sat down, pulling the computer screen to a more comfortable angle. For a moment he just sat there, then reluctantly, he began typing.

The department's IT guy down the hall could find the information he was looking for a lot quicker and wouldn't even think twice about it. Everyone in town knew AJ had come from Dallas; they would expect him to have a passing interest in a murder that had happened while he was there.

But he didn't ask the computer geek for help. He did it the semi-old-fashioned way: he used Google to look up the names of the principles in the case.

There wasn't much available, and none of it recent. A handful of stories about Teri's death, more about Israel Rodriguez's trial. He also came across a few unrelated mentions of Kinney, Myers and Taylor. That was about what he'd expected. A murdered prostitute and three cops doing their jobs didn't merit a lot of media attention.

The majority of the hits came when he looked up Masiela on Google. Cases she'd represented, bad guys she'd gotten off, victims she'd screwed over. She could have practiced any other kind of law and he wouldn't have cared, beyond thinking it was a waste of a good detective. But, no, she'd chosen criminal defense. She'd taken everything she'd learned as a cop and used it to keep perps out of jail. He never understood how defense attorneys could sleep at night, when they spent their days trying to get guilty people set free. It had been even more unforgivable with Masiela, given her years in the department.

He was about to turn away from the screen when he hesitated, hand still on the mouse. He slid it across to the small link near the top that read "Images" and clicked. Several photos loaded onto the screen: Masiela in uniform, making an arrest, walking out of the courthouse beside another guilty client after another acquittal, being honored by some local women's group, again by a Latino rights group. In most of the pictures she wore suits and her hair was pulled back and off her neck. She looked cool and elegant and successful and… satisfied.

She'd worked hard to get where she was. She had accomplished a lot. But she could have accomplished a lot of *good* instead.

Irritably, he paged away from the pictures, then called the dispatcher. "Give me the next call that comes in, will you?"

"You've got good timing, Lieutenant. I was just about to assign a shoplifting call at the mall. You want it?"

"Shoplifting?" Uniformed officers usually handled those calls.

"Yeah. A fifty-two-inch plasma TV. Almost makes me curious enough to go down there myself."

AJ laughed with him. "Yeah, I'll let you know how they managed."

It took a few minutes to get to the department store that anchored the east side of the mall. A small crowd had gathered just outside the door, where the red-faced store manager and two male clerks were holding three teenage boys. Next to them stood the television.

AJ walked around it slowly. Both of his TVs were thirty-five inches, and the biggest he'd ever owned; but this one made them look puny in comparison. He didn't even have a room in his house big enough for this TV.

Finally, he turned his attention to the boys: Connor Calloway and the Holigan brothers. If the Calloways were the social elite in the county, the Holigans were their polar opposite. Given the obvious nickname of "hooligan" several generations ago, they lived in the poorest part of town and came from broken homes with broken parents. AJ had started arresting these two when they were barely teenagers, though this was a first for Connor. Even so, AJ would bet this month's salary that stealing the TV had been Connor's idea.

The Holigans were staring at the ground, but Connor insolently met AJ's gaze. "Why'd you do this, Connor? You could have paid for that TV with your pocket change."

"What would be the fun of that?" Connor retorted, with his usual lack of respect. He was spoiled, obnoxious and rude, but everyone overlooked it because he was a Calloway and because his branch of the family had been involved in a scandal the year before that had resulted in his father's suicide.

AJ didn't give a damn that he was a Calloway, but he could cut him some slack for the suicide. Losing your father when you were seventeen, finding out that he'd loved a woman other than your mother his entire life, that he'd had a daughter with that woman and had been responsible for the mother's death and the baby's disappearance—that could be tough for anyone to deal with.

"What's the fun of going to jail?" AJ countered.

Connor sneered. "Calloways don't go to jail."

"Think again." AJ pulled his handcuffs from the case on his belt, but before he could reach for the boy's arm, a strangled noise came from the store manager.

"Uh, Detective, um…" The guy was sweating profusely now, more than the heat could account for.

"Decker," AJ said.

"Y-yes, Detective Decker. Uh, is this really necessary? I mean, it's not as if they actually made off with the TV. We can just take it back inside and—and no one has to—to go to jail, right? I mean, they're just kids."

AJ's smile was thin. The manager had called the police before he'd realized who he'd caught. If it were just the Holigans, he'd have been happy to see them dragged off in handcuffs, but a Calloway… The family members were his best customers. Most of them had turned shopping into an art form, and they didn't know the meaning of "economic downturn."

"How much does this TV cost?" he asked.

"Thirty-two-hundred dollars," one of the clerks volunteered.

"That's felony theft by taking, punishable by up to ten years in prison. You really want to let them walk because you're afraid his—" he pointed at Connor "—family won't shop here anymore?"

The manager aimed for conciliatory, but instead just sounded panicked. "Like I said, they're just kids. I—I don't want a stupid mistake to ruin their lives."

AJ rolled his eyes. "You gotta be kidding." But obviously the man wasn't. Returning the handcuffs to the case, AJ snapped it, then gestured to Connor. "Go on. Get out of here."

With a cocky smile, the kid started toward a black pickup parked at the curb—in a fire zone, no less. Not that AJ could do anything about it, since the mall was private property.

When the other boys started to follow, he stuck out his arm. "Not you two. I want to talk to you."

"But he's our ride," the younger boy whined.

"I'll give you a ride."

As the manager and the clerks began hauling the television back inside, AJ and the Holigans walked to AJ's Impala. "Where was the TV going?" he asked, as they settled inside.

Both kids kept their mouths shut for a minute, then the older one scowled. "Connor's house."

"You risked prison time to help a rich kid steal a fancy television that he could easily buy for himself? What's wrong with you two?"

"It sounded like fun," the younger cousin said defensively. "You know, it's not easy shoplifting a TV that big."

"How did you manage it?"

The kid grinned. "Connor got some girl he knew to pretend to faint in the middle of the store. While everyone was freaking out about her, we just carried the TV out the door. Pretty cool, huh?"

AJ reached across the seat to thump him on the back of the head. "You're seventeen years old; they're eighteen. You're not kids. If you'd been charged, you'd've been convicted and sent to prison. And trust me, there's nothing cool about that. And it would've been you and your brother. Not Connor. His family would never let him go to jail, and yours couldn't keep you out. You know that."

From the backseat, the older boy scowled. "He said if we got caught his family would take care of us, and they did. All that guy had to hear was his last name, and he was quick to forget all about it."

AJ scowled back. "His family didn't take care of you. You got lucky. If I'd arrested you guys, the Calloways wouldn't be hiring a lawyer for you two or coming up with bail money, either. Their only interest in you would be proving that you had somehow forced their little angel into breaking the law."

"Connor wouldn't go along with that."

"Right." AJ snorted. "He didn't even stick around to see if you needed a ride home."

They couldn't argue that. Connor hadn't even glanced back before he'd driven away.

AJ turned off River Road onto a narrow street that twisted and turned as it followed the banks of Holigan Creek. The houses they passed grew smaller and shabbier, until they reached the shabbiest of them all. A pickup sat on blocks in the front yard, and an air conditioner rattled in the window beside the door. The only sign of life was a dog stretched out in a freshly dug hole beneath an oak tree.

He turned into the soft dirt of the driveway, stopped, then faced both boys. "Look, I'd rather not see you in jail at all, but for damn sure not because of some spoiled brat like Connor Calloway and not for some stupid stunt like stealing a TV that you don't even get to watch. I know you've got brains in those thick skulls. Use them next time, would you?"

They mumbled the right words as they got out, but when AJ drove away, he heard Cate's words echoing in his head.

They didn't hear a single thing you said.

Masiela was taking a break from cleaning the doc's study when Decker came home from work. He made another brief call—"I'm coming in. Don't shoot me"—then a moment later the front door opened. She remained where she was, drinking a glass of cold-brewed tea, thinking how familiar those words were. She'd heard them the first time they'd gone to the range together; though, after seeing that she could outshoot him and every other cop there, he'd had the respect to never say them again in that situation.

She'd heard them the first time they went into a dark building on a call, and the first time they'd chased a homicide suspect into a maze of alleys and twisting streets in the middle of a late-night storm.

And she was pretty sure she'd heard them *that night,* just before he'd kissed her, when he'd unholstered her weapon and laid it aside.

Her eyes closed with the memory. She'd been drunk, but not so much as he'd thought. Not enough to forget sex with the best guy in her life.

The clunk of shoes on wood announced his approach, then he appeared in the doorway with both hands full of grocery sacks. He set them on the counter before leaving again. She began unpacking the bags, methodically grouping like items together. By the time he made his last trip—stuff she needed for stripping the shelves—she had all the cold food put away except the items needed for that evening's dinner. "Are you staying home tonight?" she asked, as he came back from the study. She held up a package of flank steaks. "I need to know how much to cook."

"Yeah, I'm in for the night."

"Barring an emergency."

He took a bottle of water from the refrigerator while she washed her hands. She half-expected him to disappear upstairs with it, but instead he sat on one of the stools. "We take call. Anything the detective on call needs help with usually goes to Tommy Maricci first. He's the one who helped me up off the ground yesterday, right after you and Donovan showed up."

She paused in the act of slicing the steak. "What were you doing on the ground?"

His expression flattened. "You didn't see? And Donovan didn't say…?"

"No. I wasn't looking." That one glimpse of Decker headed toward the police car had been more than enough for the moment. She'd been too busy after that, dealing with the pain and preparing herself for more. "What happened?"

When he didn't say anything, but his discomfort deepened, a smile spread across her face. "Did you get your ass kicked right outside the police station?"

"That would have been less painful," he said drily. He chugged half the water, then set the bottle down. "I got kicked, okay? By a fifty-something-year-old woman who weighs about ninety pounds and was well-known for kicking by everybody in the department except me."

It took a snort to stifle her laugh. "Well," she managed to say. "I guess you know now. So you got kicked in the balls and then found yourself stuck with me. Poor baby."

His hazel gaze narrowed. She knew he'd heard her use the phrase far too often to believe she was actually offering sympathy. Changing the subject, he asked, "What are you fixing?"

"Steak tacos. Okay?"

He slid to his feet, taking his water with him. "I'm easy. I'm going to change clothes and get some work done."

She watched him leave the room, his words echoing in her head. *I'm easy.*

She wished.

If forgiveness and understanding came easily to him, this next week would be much more pleasant for them both. But if forgiveness and understanding came easily, he wouldn't be the Decker who appealed to, irritated, amused and frustrated her more than any man she'd ever met.

She did a rough chop of cilantro and jalapeños, then worked them into a paste the old-fashioned way she'd learned from her grandmother: with brute force. She heard Decker come downstairs again and followed the sound of his steps into the front parlor. Music came on, almost loud enough to muffle the noise that accompanied his work.

There was a certain comfort to the scene. If Masiela let herself admit it, it was the sort of thing she had once dreamed about: she and Decker sharing a house, a life, a bed and more. Of course, in her dream, he hadn't been antagonistic and scornful. She hadn't been in hiding. Their being together had been a mutual decision.

And that dream had been a long-ago, short-lived, obviously impossible thing. It hadn't taken her long as his partner to realize that he was never going to feel that way about her. They had been buddies, both before and after *that night. Buddies* was their norm, anything else an aberration. If she hadn't been drunk, if he hadn't been…

Truth was, she didn't know what he'd been. He was stone-cold sober because she was celebrating. He'd never shown any interest in her before, had never even seemed to notice she was female, except the few times early on when he'd tried to be the macho man protecting the little woman. She'd broken him of that habit.

He hadn't been vulnerable. AJ Decker was *never* vulnerable. He'd never indulged in indiscriminate sex, though it would have been easy for him if he'd wanted to. Far easier than doing it with his partner.

She'd never known why he'd done it and never really cared.

This evening she did.

But how could she ask, when they'd both pretended for so long that it hadn't happened?

She finished making the paste and rubbed it into the meat before covering and refrigerating it. Next, she boiled red wine vinegar with sugar and jalapenos, sliced a large red onion and mixed it all together, leaving it on the counter for the flavors to meld.

After scrubbing her hands again, she went down the hall to the parlor. Decker was in the laborious process of stripping wallpaper. She gazed around the room at the cool, white marble of the fireplace, the wavy-paned window glass, the ancient chandelier overhead, but kept her distance from the windows.

"What will this room be?" she asked, finding a relatively dust-free wall to lean against.

He spared a glance from the steamer he was using to loosen the old paper. "I don't know. Mom says maybe an office or computer room."

"And you have no ideas of your own?"

He shrugged.

"I'd prefer the library for an office, but then, I come with a lot of books." She'd bet she could match the good doctor's medical library volume for volume with her law books. "You never did work much from home."

"I still don't."

"It's nice, I guess, to have the computer out of the way. Of course, when you have kids, you have to watch them like hawks while they're online."

The muscles tightened in his neck at the mention of children. Had he decided, along with the house and possibly marriage, that he wanted kids after all, or was he still not feeling the need to create little Deckers? Did the doctor want babies, or would it interfere with her career? It wasn't Masiela's business, any of it, but she had always thought that Decker never having children would be a shame.

"I saw you cleaned the library."

"I did. The room was pretty spooky. There were cobwebs in every corner—and I'm including the ones under every single shelf. You haven't done much in there since you moved in, have you?"

"Nope. I work forty-plus hours a week. I take call, right along with my detectives. I'm on a couple of committees here in town, and I like to kick back and do nothing once in a while. Oh yeah, and I work on this place. I don't have the energy to clean."

"Don't get testy," she teased. "Tell me again why you bought this house."

"The timing was right."

"So you were getting serious about Dr. Cate. This house came on the market. She liked it…"

He twisted to give her a long, steady look. It was hard to hold his gaze, but she forced herself, looking for some hint of how close she'd come to the truth. She couldn't find it, not in his eyes, not in the flat line of his mouth. She couldn't tell if he was annoyed by her prying, or if he felt anything at all beyond resignation that he had to put up with her.

Finally he turned back to his task. "Only little kids and white-haired old ladies call her Dr. Cate," he said, his voice as flat as his expression. "And your timer's beeping."

Faintly, over the music, she heard the *beep-beep* and shoved herself away from the door frame. "I'll call you when dinner's ready."

* * *

How did she found out Cate's name? AJ wondered about this as he scraped off a thick wad of paper with more force than was necessary. Yeah, he had her business card taped inside the cabinet door, along with a half-dozen others, but Masiela hadn't assumed he was dating any of *them*.

Must have been the delivery kid from Luigi's. He'd mentioned "the doc." Masiela knew he was seeing someone, then she'd seen the card. "Gee, she ought to be a detective," he muttered.

Then the sarcasm faded. Really, she should. She had good instincts. She looked at things differently from most male cops, himself included, and she never focused on the obvious suspect without still keeping an eye on the not-so-obvious ones, too.

So why didn't he ask her what she'd found in the Rodriguez case?

He had his reasons. One: he knew everyone involved—the cops, the killer, the victim—way better than Masiela did.

Two: he knew the details of the case as well as anyone. Reliable witnesses had put Rodriguez in the area with Teri that night, arguing with her on a street corner six blocks away, still arguing at a diner two blocks away, then, ten minutes after her death, alone in his car, stopped for a defective taillight eight blocks away.

Three: he knew that Teri had wanted out of the prostitution business. She'd wanted to move away and make a fresh start with her little girl. AJ had warned her not to tell Rodriguez, to just disappear one day. He'd offered her money to do it. Not enough—saving hadn't been high on his priority list back then—but enough to get them out of town. But she'd told the pimp anyway in some misguided attempt to be fair.

Four: AJ knew Rodriguez wasn't the kind to let a girl go easily. The last one who'd tried had been beaten to death, her face so battered that her own mother couldn't recognize her.

Five: he knew that Masiela's focus had changed. She wasn't one of the good guys anymore. She'd stopped caring about right and wrong and justice. He'd watched her in the courtroom a few times—had seen how her face lit up when she came up against one of her former fellow detectives on the witness stand. He'd watched her manipulate witnesses into saying things that weren't true and juries into believing things that weren't said.

She'd been one hell of a detective. But that Masiela, the one who'd been his partner and best friend, was gone. He knew that too well.

Slowly, he became aware of an aroma drifting on the air—rich, savory, spicy—and his stomach growled. His kitchen had never smelled that good, not even when he was heating one of his mother's casseroles. Setting his tools aside, he went into the bathroom to wash up, then followed the scent into the kitchen.

Masiela's back was to him as she cooked steak slices in a hot skillet, and she was moving to music only she could hear—literally, he saw, when he sat down at the counter and glimpsed the thin, white wire of an earbud threading through her hair. Spread across the counter in front of him was the rest of the meal: guacamole, chunky the way he liked it, along with tortilla chips, sour cream, diced tomatoes, shredded cheddar and a bowl of limp, red onion slices. He fished one out and bit into it, and damned if it didn't bite back. That was when he saw the jalapeño slices in the bowl.

With her long hair swaying and her hips doing the same, she managed to match half of the description "domestic goddess." She had curves, which men weren't supposed to appreciate under current fashion standards, but everyone he knew did. Especially him. Her breasts were full, her waist narrow, her hips nicely flared. And those legs…sexy woman runner legs.

Damn.

This was Masiela, he reminded himself. *Ex*-partner, *ex*-friend, defense lawyer, traitor. *Stop looking at her and think about Cate instead.*

Trouble was, Masiela was right there in front of him, and wasn't an easy woman to ignore.

She transferred the meat to a cutting board that he hadn't known he owned, turned—and was startled. With her free hand, she pulled the earbuds out and a tinny version of the make-your-ears-hurt music she preferred became audible. "I didn't realize you were there."

"I came to see what smelled so good." His stomach growled again, giving credence to the words.

"It's almost ready. The meat has to rest a minute while I warm the tortillas." She opened a plastic bag and pulled out a half-dozen tortillas, then browned them, one by one, in a second hot skillet. By the time she'd wrapped them in a warm towel, sliced the meat and set two bottles of beer on the counter, he was all but drooling.

The first bite was amazing and reminded him of something his father had routinely said since AJ was a kid. *If you find a woman who can cook as well as your mama, marry her.* Carol Ann had always flushed with pleasure, then swatted at him, murmuring, *Oh, Adam.*

But damned if AJ hadn't found a woman who cooked even better than his mother.

When he could talk again, he asked, "Is this recipe from one of your grandmothers?"

"No. I saw it on TV a few years ago and have been making it ever since."

"How are the old ladies?"

"Aging better than any of us have a right to." She sprinkled a few shreds of cheese over her taco. "They're roommates in an assisted living place in Dallas. Can you imagine that?"

AJ chuckled. Her grandmothers hadn't actually disliked each other. It was just that each had wanted to be her grandchildren's favorite. The competition had sometimes gotten fierce, but Masiela had never let them force her into a choice. One was her favorite Cuban grandmother, she'd always said, and the other was her favorite Mexican grandmother.

"My parents had more trouble working out a visitation schedule for them than they did for us kids when they divorced," Masiela went on. "Mom's okay with running into Dad's wife there. She just doesn't want to see *him.*"

"If my grandmothers had ever been forced to share quarters, one of them would have cut off the other's oxygen. Mom's mother never believed Dad was good enough for her daughter, and Dad's mother never forgave her for it."

"And your parents have been together how long now?"

He stopped to do the math. "Forty-five years. Plus the five years they dated first."

They had a good marriage, the kind he'd always figured he would have someday. They still lived in the house they bought after he was born, four blocks from his paternal grandparents and a mile from his mother's folks. They still attended the same church they got married in, still organized every family reunion, still worried about their kids and now their grandkids.

They were still in love, maybe not as passionately as forty-five years ago, but more deeply.

Though he'd been considering marriage to Cate, he wasn't in love with her now. What were the odds he would be in forty-five years? In five years?

Not something he wanted to consider.

"So parents don't always know what's best for their children." Masiela finished off her taco, took a tortilla from the towel and began assembling another. "I was just starting to date when Mom and Dad divorced, so she's never given me advice on men. She says her judgment was so obviously flawed that I'd be better off making my own mistakes instead of listening to her."

"She's still holding a bit of a grudge, huh?"

Her response was the snort AJ expected. He'd met Carmen Leal a few times and found her pretty, intelligent and about as self-absorbed as they came. He'd figured credit for Masiela's normalcy went to her grandmothers and Masiela herself.

"She's not bugging you for grandkids?" He made another taco, too, easily double the size of hers. She would stop after the second one and munch on chips and guacamole while he polished off everything else.

At the moment, AJ couldn't remember if Cate even liked guacamole.

"The only kids Mom is interested in now have been dead for a thousand years. She sees Yelina's girls maybe twice a year. Whatever maternal instincts she had were used up with us."

Though Masiela's expression remained unchanged, there was something sad in her voice. Regret that her kids wouldn't have the kind of grandmother she had? He couldn't imagine it. Grandma Bolton might not have cared much for his dad, but she'd loved his kids every bit as fiercely as Grandma Decker had, every bit as fiercely as Masiela's grandmothers had loved her.

"I'll just have to do what Yelina did—find a man with a large enough family that the kids don't notice someone is missing. Her husband is one of nine kids, and they all live within an hour's drive of their parents' house."

I live less than thirty minutes from my parents, both sisters and their families, assorted aunts and uncles and uncounted cousins.

The thought came from nowhere and damn near made him squirm. It wasn't as if he was offering himself as a candidate. He'd *never* thought of her that way.

Except for the night he found himself with his arms around her and his tongue down her throat. He'd thought of her a lot of ways then, mostly naked. But once he regained his sanity, the only time he'd wanted to touch her was to protect her or to smack some sense into her.

All he wanted now was to get through the next six days without a problem, then to see the last of her, for good this time.

Swear to God, that was the *only* thing he wanted from Masiela.

Chapter 5

Masiela sat at one end of the couch, her feet tucked beneath her, and AJ occupied the other end, legs stretched out and disreputable sneakers propped on the coffee table. He had control of the remote and had finally settled on a baseball game. Not the most exciting game in the world, but it beat watching fishing.

She expected him to go back to work in the front parlor after dinner, to leave her on her own again until bedtime, but he showed no such inclination. Maybe this was his "once in a while" to kick back and do nothing. And he was relaxed enough to do it with her.

She warned herself not to make too much of that fact. It wasn't as if he'd really chosen her company. He was just making the best of a bad situation. As she was.

Right.

For distraction, she eased to her feet and padded into the kitchen. "Want some cookies?"

"Nah. But grab me a Coke, would you?"

She took two cans of pop from the refrigerator, set them on the coffee table, then returned to the counter. The first cookie went straight into her mouth, and, while munching, she shook three more onto a saucer. After a moment's thought to her recent lack of exercise, she returned one to the bag, picked up the saucer and was turning to leave the kitchen when an explosion sounded. Glass shattered, both outside and in, as the plate slid from her suddenly limp fingers, crashing to the floor.

"Get down!" As she dropped to all fours, AJ jumped to his feet and dashed from the room, thudding up the stairs to get the weapon he'd left there.

The room was darker than it had been seconds ago, and between the rapid thuds of her heartbeat, she realized why: the security light outside was dark. Had it blown out due to some sort of power surge…or had someone shot it out?

AJ's footsteps pounded down the stairs, then the front door quietly closed. Avoiding the shards of glass, Masiela crawled across the kitchen floor and into the dining room, then plopped onto her butt in an interior corner, unholstered her weapon and sat straining to hear anything besides her own fright. All she could pick up were normal sounds.

She should be out there backing up AJ, searching in the dark. In all the years they'd worked together, she'd never let him go into a dangerous situation alone. If it was his old buddies out there, it would be three against one—three who played dirty against one who didn't. They wouldn't hesitate to kill him if he stood between them and her, and she couldn't bear to have that on her conscience.

Her body trembled as she pushed to her feet. Back in the day, she'd always been gung ho, into the fray, kick ass and take names. Foot chases had been fun; felony take-downs had gotten her heart pumping; she'd never shied away from getting physical with a suspect, even if he was twice her size. The first time she was shot at, she'd been so pumped with adrenaline that it had taken hours to come down.

The second time, she'd had too much to drink and wound up in bed with Decker.

But back in the day, it had always been business. The bad guys hadn't had anything against her, just the badge she wore.

This was personal.

She moved through the dimly lit dining and living rooms, reaching the front door in seconds. Steadier now, she slowly twisted the door knob, opening it with only the slightest of sounds. Standing in the shadows, she nudged the door with her foot to swing it back, brought the pistol up to firing position and stepped into the doorway, then abruptly lowered it again.

AJ was coming up the steps, gripping a battered baseball in his left hand, managing to look both relieved and grim at the same time. He tossed it to her before turning to secure the door, and she looked at it. It was well worn, the writing rubbed off, nothing special and impossible to trace.

Unless you knew where to look.

"Kid I had a run-in with today was star pitcher on the Copper Lake High School team three years straight. I had to let him go, but he still wasn't happy with me."

She felt a surprisingly strong sense of relief. If their visitor had been merely a vandal, his intent to do property damage, there was no need to call the police. No need to pack up and run.

"Arrogant punk." At his raised brow, she shrugged. "He didn't bother to take the ball with him when he left."

"He probably wanted me to know it was him, but not be able to prove it." AJ headed to the back of the house, stopping in the laundry room for a broom and dust pan. On his way to the kitchen, he glanced at her. "You weren't actually planning to go outside, were you?"

Her only answer was a level look.

"Remember the rules you agreed to yesterday? You don't go out. You stay out of sight."

She snorted. "And what if it'd been Kinney and the others out there? I might have had to save your ass."

Now it was his turn to give the flat, steady look.

Irritably she tried to take the broom from him. "My mess. I'll clean up."

"You're bleeding. Take care of that."

Glancing down, she saw blood smeared on her left hand. Apparently, she hadn't avoided all the broken glass when crawling from the kitchen. She went to the bathroom and washed the tiny nick, not even bad enough for a bandage, and thought of what AJ had said. *He probably wanted me to know it was him, but not be able to prove it.*

That, she'd always thought, was one reason why so many people had been willing to believe that Israel Rodriguez killed Teri Riggs. Everyone had *known* he'd killed the other prostitute when she tried to leave the life, but no one could prove it. They'd had to watch him get away with murder, and that had eaten at every cop who'd ever had contact with him.

But avoiding prison when he was guilty didn't justify sending him there when he was innocent.

And he *was* innocent of Teri's murder. Masiela was staking her life on it.

AJ came downstairs Wednesday morning to the smell of freshly brewed coffee and to Masiela eating cookies at the counter with her own cup beside her. She didn't look as if the little excitement last night had affected her in any way. In fact, she looked sleepy. Soft. Sexy.

She glanced at his clothes—gray trousers, white shirt, gray tie—but didn't comment. He explained anyway. "I've got to go to court this morning. The defense counsel can show up in shorts and a T-shirt, but the judge wants the rest of us in uniforms or suits."

"Let me guess: the defense counsel is a Calloway."

His brows raised slightly. "Yeah. Robbie. One of the better of the bunch."

She feigned shock with her hand to her heart and her eyes wide. "You actually have something good to say about a defense lawyer?"

He frowned, but there wasn't much annoyance behind it. "In any group, someone's got to be the best and someone's got to be the worst. Of the Calloways in general and the Calloway lawyers in particular, Robbie's one of the best."

There was more to it than that, and they both knew it. Robbie had already been a lawyer when AJ met him. He'd never been a cop. He'd never planned to become a prosecutor, and in a small town like Copper Lake, criminal law was only a part of his practice.

And the biggest reason AJ could cut Robbie some slack and not her: they'd never been partners, buddies, a part of each other's lives. He'd never felt betrayed by Robbie.

"Have fun. Hope the right side wins."

Hope the good guys win. That was what she used to say before court appearances. Back then, the good guys had always been the cops. Now...

Giving her a narrow look, he picked up his coffee and left.

Like any cop, he had his favorite duties and his least favorite. Testifying in court ranked near the top of the least favorite. There had been worse things—getting shot at, watching Morgan Riggs at her mother's funeral, having to tell parents that their sixteen-year-old son had been killed. But in the day-to-day routine, court appearances annoyed him. Defense attorneys annoyed him, even the ones he liked, like Robbie Calloway and Jamie Munroe Calloway.

Especially the one he *used* to like, before she'd turned to the dark side.

Once the hearing was over, he walked out of the courthouse with Robbie, stopping at the bottom of the steps. "How's the house going?" Robbie asked.

"Slowly." Unlike AJ, all the Calloway brothers were good with their hands. Russ had his construction company, and all four of them rebuilt old junk heaps for fun. "How's the kid?"

Robbie grinned. "Looking more like his mama every day."

"Thank God for that." Anamaria Calloway was quite possibly the most beautiful woman AJ had ever met. She and Robbie might not have been an obvious match, but they had an abundance of the passion AJ's parents had shared, that he and Cate couldn't manage for even one night.

"Hey, we're playing poker tonight—Mitch, Russ, Tommy and Ty. If you want to lose a few bucks—"

The blare of a horn, followed by the squeal of tires, interrupted Robbie's invitation, and they both turned in time to see a glossy silver Mustang swerve into a parked car, cut back into traffic, then crash into another car across the street. The passenger, looking dazed, remained in the car, but the driver opened the door, staggered a few steps, then took off at a trot.

AJ recognized him at the same time Robbie muttered, "Oh, crap. That damn moron."

AJ flashed a grin as he handed his suit coat to Robbie. "Hold on to this. I've gotta catch this guy. I owe him one."

Connor Calloway was possibly shaken up from the crash, intoxicated or high—or merely, as his cousin put it, a damn moron. What he wasn't, despite being half AJ's age and better dressed for a run in shorts and sneakers, was a good runner. AJ closed steadily on him, then made a flying tackle.

The kid hit the ground hard, yelping like a girl as their combined weights skidded him forward on the pavement a foot or so. Concrete didn't make for a soft landing. Neither did 185 pounds hitting square in his back.

"What are you doing?" Connor demanded. "Get the hell off me. I'll have your badge for this. Do you freakin' *know* who I am?"

AJ raised to his knees, pulled the boy's arms behind him and handcuffed him none too gently, then stood and lifted him to his feet. "You bet I know who you are. Connor Calloway, you're under arrest. You have the right—"

Connor jerked around to look at him and sneered. "This is harassment. I'm gonna sue your ass and the whole freakin' police department. I'm gonna—"

"Shut up, Connor."

The kid's sneer widened when Robbie joined them. "This is my lawyer. Get your hands off me and take off those cuffs *now,* or you're gonna be in so damn much trouble—"

"Shut up, Connor," Robbie repeated sharply. "What the hell do you think you're doing? You totaled three cars, you could have hurt your passenger, you could have killed someone. Were you even thinking?"

AJ kept a straight face. From what he'd heard, Robbie and his brothers had been their generation's Connor. They'd been in and out of trouble for years, with nothing but the family name to keep them from going to jail. "High-spirited," people said about them. But there was something mean-spirited about Connor, something that hinted of deeper trouble.

"You can't talk to me like that," Connor said. "You're my lawyer."

"Lawyer?" Robbie chuckled. "Hell, I'm volunteering to be a witness for the prosecution. After you get booked into jail, call your uncle Seth. Maybe he'll take care of you."

Connor fell into sullen silence, and AJ finished reading him his rights as a patrol car pulled alongside them. The officer put the boy in the backseat, then drove away.

He and Robbie started back toward the court house. "On behalf of the family—at least most of them—sorry about that."

AJ gazed at him as Robbie handed over his jacket. "Did you know he got caught shoplifting a thirty-two-hundred-dollar television yesterday, but the store manager wouldn't press charges because he's one of you? And I can't prove it, but I think he threw a baseball and broke my security light last night."

"Kid's got a hell of an arm." Robbie grimaced. "He gets a lot of breaks because he's a Calloway and because of his dad's death. Obviously, he's not learning from them."

"Maybe he needs some other kind of breaks. A few lessons in how to be a man, in accepting the consequences of his actions, maybe a little counseling."

"Good luck with that. He hasn't seen his mother in years. He's living with his stepmom, who takes just enough responsibility to maintain access to the family money. He doesn't want anything to do with our side of the family, especially now that I'm married to Anamaria, unless it somehow benefits him."

Connor's father had killed himself over Anamaria's mother, Glory, and Connor and Anamaria shared a half-sister, if anyone ever managed to find her. A half-sister who, like Anamaria, was of mixed race. Tough for some wealthy white Southerners to accept.

"He's going to self-destruct unless someone steps in," AJ said mildly.

Robbie acknowledged him with a grim nod as they reached the accident scene. Traffic was being rerouted at the nearest intersections, and wreckers vied for space among the police cars and the lone ambulance to hook up to the three vehicles.

"God, I'm glad I'm not in traffic anymore," AJ said. "See you."

He was in his Impala, fastening his seat belt, when he noticed the stain on his left sleeve: something brown and tarry on the outside, a bit of red seeping through from the inside. When he'd tackled Connor, his left arm had been under the kid, scraping along the pavement. A stained shirt sleeve and raw skin were a fair trade for the pleasure of arresting the kid, even if it did mean going home to change.

Even if it meant seeing Masiela. Maybe still wearing that bit of nothing she slept in.

He notified the dispatcher of his destination as he headed that way. The neighborhood was quiet—the norm for hot summer days. He couldn't remember a day when he was growing up that had been too hot for playing outside, but the kids who lived around him seemed to be more delicate. They required air conditioning, computers and video games to make it through the summer months.

The only exception was the little girl next door. She sat on the top porch step, surrounded by dolls and stuffed animals, murmuring to them in tones too low for him to understand when he got out of the car.

"Hey, Calie," he called as he reached his own steps. He'd been saying hello to her ever since he'd learned her name. The first dozen times she'd run inside the house and slammed the door. For a while, she'd held her ground, giving him a flat stare way too old for someone her age. Today, for the first time, she lifted the bear she was cradling and waggled his paw in a wave.

AJ was so surprised that he dropped his keys when he pulled them from the lock. Who knew? In another year or two, she might actually speak to him.

As he opened the door, he bent to pick up the keys. He started to straighten, when a familiar sensation prickled the hairs on his neck. Sixth sense, caution, danger... the feeling he'd often gotten when clearing buildings or serving warrants. His gaze shifted slowly to a pair of battered sneakers in the living room doorway, traveling up over tanned legs and stained shorts, stopping on the .40-caliber pistol pointed at him. Masiela's aim was rock-steady. He'd never seen her tremble or hesitate, not even when the bad guys' shots were coming too close for comfort.

"Gee," he said quietly. "Guess I should have called."

She lowered the weapon, then holstered it as he walked through the door. "I wasn't expecting you for another five or six hours."

"I need to change clothes." He raised his left arm so she could see for herself. If he were showing blood stains to Cate, she'd be rolling up his sleeve, calling for antiseptics and antibiotics and bandages, making enough of a fuss to let him know she cared.

Masiela, on the other hand, wasn't impressed. "I hope this wasn't another fifty-some-year-old woman who weighed ninety pounds."

"Nope, this was the eighteen-year-old baseball-throwing punk who's gonna sue my ass."

She smiled at that. Between them, they couldn't count the number of times they'd heard that threat from a disgruntled citizen. Or "I'll have your badge." Sixteen years, and he'd never once gotten sued or lost his badge.

"Let me know if he does sue," Masiela said as she started down the hall. "I'll quit working on the library immediately. There's no way a kid would appreciate my efforts."

He watched until she turned into the room. Not for any particular reason. Not because there was anything at all interesting about the way she moved. He was just giving the adrenaline time to drain away.

Yeah, that was what he told himself.

Thinking he deserved one more of Willie's kicks, he went upstairs to change into khakis and another polo shirt. The scrape on his arm was nothing to worry about. He cleaned and bandaged it, then tossed his shirt into the hamper.

What he should have done when he got back downstairs was yell, "I'm leaving now," and followed through. What he did instead was turn down the hall toward the library.

The windows in there were open, with a fan blowing toward them, removing some of the chemical stink from the room. The odds of exposure there were slim. Inside looking out, the only view was the neighbor's blank wall. Outside looking in, crape myrtle branches created a dense screen for anyone shorter than six-and-a-half feet tall.

Masiela was standing in front of the fan. It blew her damp shirt against her, a detail he noted only because he was a good detective, and dried the sweat that dotted her face.

"Nice work," he commented. She'd accomplished a lot in the few hours he'd been gone, evidenced by one empty can of stripper, a pile of dirty cloths and a dozen or more shelves scraped down to bare wood. It was mind-numbing work for someone who hated tedium—though apparently not as much as she hated daytime TV.

His phone vibrated and he pulled it from the case clipped to his belt. After a glance at the caller ID—it was the chief—he grimly flipped it open. "Decker."

Masiela turned her back to the fan, giving the impression of privacy. He listened to his boss, made the appropriate responses and wondered how a pair of plain denim shorts, not too short or too snug, could look so damn enticing.

"Yes, sir," he said at last. "I'll be there in five minutes, sir."

She turned around again when he ended the call. "Trouble?"

"Nah. It's just that the kid I arrested this morning is a Calloway. Arresting one of them always requires some damage control."

Her expression tightened just a fraction at the mention of the Calloway name. Like most cops, she disliked people whose name was more important than their crimes. At least, she had when she *was* a cop.

After she'd become a defense attorney...

His own jaw tightened as he put the phone back in the case, then turned toward the door. "I'll be home between four and five. Don't knock yourself out in here until I find out if the kid's already sued me."

A glance over his shoulder showed her faint smile as she returned to the half-finished shelf.

Taking a break for lunch, Masiela settled on the couch with the last pieces of leftover pizza and a glass of iced tea and flipped through the TV channels. Nothing, nothing, nothing. Choosing a channel at random, she took a bite of cold cheese and veggies and chewed slowly. She missed the light that would be flooding the room if she weren't being such a scaredy girl, though not the heat the afternoon sun brought with it.

Her gaze strayed to the corner where she'd left her laptop case. Her cell phone was tucked inside, powered off, so the GPS unit couldn't be used to locate her. The laptop was off, too. She couldn't check her voicemails or e-mails, couldn't risk the chance that Myers and his buds had circumvented the legal process and gained access to her Internet or cell accounts. No doubt there were messages from Yelina and Elian on one device or the other, from her father and her grandmothers, from her office and probably from the cops who'd sent her into hiding. She had told her family she would be out of touch but safe, but they would worry anyway.

I hated when you were a cop, Yelina had said. *I never thought you'd be in more danger now than then.*

Neither had she, Masiela thought, with a grim smile.

Lunch done, she went back to work in the library. After the stripping and the sanding were finished, every piece of wood would be uniformly smooth. AJ would stain it, and one day Dr. Cate would fill the shelves with books and whatever kind of knickknacks a Calloway woman acquired. She would give AJ the credit for her beautiful office, and he would never tell her differently, because he wouldn't want to explain that he'd hidden a woman he'd once slept with under her nose for a week.

Funny. Masiela had never really imagined AJ marrying, and certainly not into the most influential and powerful family in town. He'd had a solidly middle-class upbringing; he wasn't impressed by money or power; he preferred jeans and T-shirts over dressier clothes and a pizza joint over a country club.

He must love Dr. Cate a lot.

Masiela's jaw clenched, and she was pretty sure it didn't relax until 4:29, when the phone rang. She didn't get up from the floor, but she did stop scraping long enough to hear Decker's message on the kitchen answering machine. "I'm here. Don't shoot."

She looked awful. She was hot and sweaty and had stripper gunk under all her nails. Her clothes were dirty, her ponytail had gone limp hours ago and she ached pretty much everywhere. It was a good thing she wasn't trying to impress anyone.

The front door opened and closed, then footsteps climbed the stairs. His bedroom was directly above the library; an occasional creak allowed her to track his movements around the room. He would strip down to his boxers—unless Dr. Cate preferred some other kind of underwear—and change into shorts and a T-shirt, probably something really old and ratty. He never threw a favorite shirt away, not until it literally fell apart.

She knew so damn much about him, and he about her, and yet he still believed Myers and the others over her. The unfairness of it all would drag her low if she let it.

Footsteps descended the stairs, then stopped in the doorway. "Knock it off for the day," he said, his voice low, just this side of gravelly. "Come have a beer."

Concentrating on not looking at him, she considered declining, but a spasm in her right hand changed her mind. "I'll be out in a minute."

He left—she felt the change in the air—and she wiped away the last of the stripper from the shelf. After cleaning the putty knife, she sealed the can, stood and stretched, long and slow, bending at the waist to ease the kinks out of her back. Her hair fell forward, her fingertips brushing the floor, and the air shifted again. Looking between her feet planted wide apart on the wood floor, she saw an upside-down version of Decker, two beers in hand and a look on his face of...

It was masculine appreciation for a female body. No big deal. He'd always admired her determination to maintain the fitness she'd attained in the academy. The stronger and more capable she was, the better she could do her job and the safer they both were.

It was the blood rushing to her head that made her

cheeks hot, not his gaze. Slowly she straightened, and everything—her hair, her shirt, her shorts, her view of the world—slid back into place.

"Thanks," she said, taking one of the beers as she passed him. She gulped a swallow on her way to the sink. After scrubbing up, she slid onto one of the stools at the counter. He took the other. "How did the damage control go?"

"Not bad. It helped that Connor's cousin, Robbie, witnessed the whole thing." The corner of his mouth quirked up. "Another cousin by marriage, Jamie, is the department's lawyer."

"Good grief, how many Calloways are there?"

"No one knows. And they reproduce like rabbits." The partial smile turned into a full one. "Most of them are okay. There's just the bunch that thinks being a Calloway makes them better than everyone else."

"Must be nice. Did the chief want to drop the charges?"

"Nope. Just wanted my side of the story before he talked to the kid's lawyer. He totaled three cars in front of the courthouse, then fled. There isn't much else to say, except the kid's claiming I'm harassing him because I almost arrested him for shoplifting a big-screen plasma TV yesterday."

"Almost? The store owner wouldn't press charges against a Calloway?" she asked drily.

Decker nodded. "Can you imagine what your parents would have done if you'd pulled a stunt like that?"

"I'd still be grounded."

"I'd probably be dead."

She nodded. "Your father's strict moral code." Both his parents, but his father in particular, had taught Decker all the important lessons, practically from the cradle:

honesty, honor, courage, trustworthiness, responsibility. They weren't just words, they were who he was. How he lived his life. Not embracing those concepts would be impossible for him.

Too bad he'd learned wrongheaded loyalty and stubbornness just as well.

"So…" She took another drink. "How does Dr. Cate fit in with Connor, Robbie, Jamie and all the other little bunnies?" She didn't sound *too* interested, did she? Just casually so, she hoped.

"Cate's divorced from one of Robbie's cousins." He sounded as flat as she was afraid her question had been.

So the good doctor had married into the family, then divorced out of it but kept the name. Probably kept some of the prestige, too, along with a hefty chunk of her ex's Calloway money.

And now she was in line to marry into a better family.

Some people had all the luck.

Chapter 6

 Why had she asked about Cate? AJ wondered. Not just once but a couple times. She'd never shown much interest in the women he dated, even though they'd doubled a lot. She said that she'd learned all she needed to know from the first one. After that, only the names changed; everything else—body type, character, personality—stayed the same.

 And the hell of it was, she'd been right. He picked a type and stuck with it: pretty, empty-headed, superficial. Not likely to challenge him anywhere except in bed. Not likely to inspire anything deeper in him besides short-term fondness and lust.

 Not likely to remind him even remotely of Masiela. After all, who wanted to go to bed at night with a woman who reminded him of his buddy?

 He snorted silently. Yeah, right, that was all Masiela had been—just a buddy. He could let himself pretend that. After all, only he knew, and he already knew he was a fool. The proof sat across the counter from him.

"Hey." Masiela snapped her fingers in front of his face, startling him from his thoughts. "For the second time, have you heard from Donovan?"

He blinked, then shook his head. "You know Donovan. He works on a need-to-know basis."

"Considering that I'm the one who's been threatened, I think I have a pretty good need to know what's going on."

"He'll call when he's got something."

Donovan worked cases the way he played poker: with his cards close to his chest. He wasn't the type to check in just to say there was nothing to say.

"So at least I can be fairly sure my condo hasn't been torched or my office blown up."

"Yeah, like that's gonna happen."

She stared at him, her face expressionless. "When they shot out the window, I was standing right there. I got cut by the flying glass." She stuck out her left arm, her right index finger pointing from one small line to the next. Scars, thin and pale against her bronzed skin, stretching in broken lines from the back of her hand to her shoulder. "They broke into my house. They threatened me."

She paused, and his muscles stiffened. He knew what was coming next, and damn it, he didn't want to hear it. He slid from the bar stool, but had barely gained his feet when she said it, flatly, as if it couldn't be anything but true.

"They threw Teri Riggs off that building."

He stared back, heat and anger building inside him. He hadn't been working that night, but the news got to him pretty quickly. He'd gone to the scene; he'd seen Teri's body, broken and bloodied, on the sidewalk. She'd been a little thing—five-three, not even a hundred pounds—but she'd had a big smile and big dreams. She'd had plans for herself and her little girl, plans that AJ had been encouraging for two years. Plans that had died along with her, at the end of a five-story fall.

"Why?" He barely managed to force the word out. "What in hell did Myers, Kinney and Taylor have to gain by killing Teri?"

"They got her pimp locked up on a life sentence."

"You're saying they killed her just to see Rodriguez in prison?" AJ shook his head. "You think Teri died because she just happened to be in the wrong place at the wrong time? That three dedicated and decorated officers murdered her just so they could frame her pimp? Jeez, Mas! You *know* these guys. They were our buddies, our friends!"

She stood, too, arms folded over her middle. "Buddies? Who are you kidding, Decker? They harassed me from the day I joined the squad. Touching, leering, making suggestive comments. They cornered me when I was alone, rubbing against me, telling me they had just what I needed, so I made damn sure I wasn't alone around them. When they backed us on calls, if you were out of sight, so was my backer. Remember the time I got the black eye?"

He did. They had met for dinner and walked in on a robbery in progress. He'd gone after one suspect, Myers and Taylor after another, and Masiela and Kinney had run out the back door after the third. They'd met up again, prisoners in tow, and she had bruises on the whole right side of her face. Kinney said she'd outrun him, that by the time he'd caught up, the suspect had already punched her, and she hadn't disputed him.

"He stood there and watched that guy come after me. He didn't step in. He didn't help. He just watched."

"I don't believe you." But the memory nagged at him. When she and Kinney had returned with their prisoner, her usual euphoria of a chase and an arrest had been absent, buried beneath something else. Decker had thought maybe it was a sobering experience: the first time a suspect had almost come out ahead in a struggle. A lesson that all the training in the world couldn't ensure she would always prevail.

A lesson he'd thought she needed, to rein in her enthusiasm. She'd been so damn convinced that she was invincible. She'd never been afraid, but he'd been afraid sometimes for her. He thought she'd learned there was no such thing as invincibility that night and had luckily survived to tell the tale.

But it appeared she'd learned a different, more bitter lesson.

"Detective Kinney stood by and let a suspect beat the crap out of me," she said quietly. "You can deny it, but it doesn't change the facts."

"If they harassed you, if they failed to back you up, why didn't you tell someone? Why didn't you file a complaint against them?" He hesitated, preferring to keep the words inside, but letting them slip out anyway. "Why didn't you tell *me?*"

Her mouth shifted into a sneer. "File a complaint? You're kidding, right? Cops don't 'file complaints' against other cops, not unless they're looking to end their own careers. You know how narrow-minded cops are when it comes to their own. Everyone in the whole damn department would have made my life miserable. I would have been ostracized and eventually forced out."

"So what? You were planning to quit anyway. If what

you're saying is true, why not try to take them down on your way out? Why wait until now?"

For a long time, she looked at him as if she hardly knew him. Finally, in a flat, accusing voice, she said, "I'm going to take a shower, then I'll start dinner."

He let her get as far as the doorway before he responded. "Don't bother. I'm going out."

She paused at his words, only for a beat or two, then continued down the hall without looking back.

He picked up his empty beer bottle, his fingers clenching around the long neck. He'd like to throw it, listen to it explode, watch the shards burst into the air before falling. But he wasn't the type to break things. Besides, he'd just have to sweep it all up when he was done. Been there, done that the night before.

He'd told Masiela he was going out, and though there was nowhere he wanted to go, he felt obligated to follow through. When the shower came on upstairs, he knew the last thing he needed was to stay down here and imagine her up there, taking off her clothes, stepping into the tub, being naked and wet....

He set the bottle in the recycling bin under the sink, grabbed his keys off the counter and left the house. The temperature was somewhere around ninety-two, and the air was thick with humidity that made breathing a chore. Next door, Calie sat in a rocker, surrounded by dolls, and her brother was sprawled in the next chair. Their lives had started out tougher than his and probably wouldn't be improving any time soon. He'd been damned lucky to have the upbringing he had, though he felt right now as if all the bad luck he'd avoided in his life was piling up around him. A whole lot of trouble in one fairly slender package.

He just drove, no destination in mind. He turned off

the music he usually listened to and tried to let his mind wander, but it kept wandering back to his house.

He didn't believe Masiela's story about their fellow detectives. Not that he thought she was deliberately lying. Maybe she'd let her animosity toward Kinney and the others color the way she read the situations. Maybe she was seeing hostility where, in reality, there'd been none. Maybe…

Maybe she was telling the truth.

They'd picked on her from the beginning—the same sort of hazing they'd subjected every newbie to. They'd made assumptions about her abilities, and they'd given her a hard time. But after Decker had taken her on as a partner, all that had stopped. At least, he'd thought so.

Now she was saying it hadn't stopped, but had escalated to the point that they'd refused to back her up. A cop without backup could easily get killed. Would the men he knew put another cop in that kind of danger?

He couldn't imagine it. Didn't want to believe it.

But some small part of him knew it was possible.

Some smaller part believed she was telling the truth—about that, at least. But killing Teri Riggs? No way. Hazing and harassment, okay, maybe. But cold-blooded murder? It hadn't happened. It *couldn't* have.

After a while, he pulled into a drive-in in the next town for a greasy burger. The aroma of fried onions stayed with him all the way back to Copper Lake.

He stopped at the edge of town, at a small bar set at the back of a gravel parking lot. It wasn't the sort of place he normally went to drink; he was more likely to see people that he'd arrested in the squat, cinder block building than anyone he socialized with. A good reason for going there tonight. He didn't want to be social.

He picked up a beer at the bar, then settled at a table

near the television mounted high on the wall. It was tuned to a baseball game, though none of the patrons appeared interested. They sat in small groups or alone, a few watching him, the rest focusing on their drinks and whatever problem had brought them in tonight.

He didn't want to think about his problem. He would have to face her again soon enough.

He finished the beer and ordered another. By the time it was gone, the game was over, everyone had lost interest in him, and he was damn near cross-eyed with the need for sleep.

He stood, his joints creaking with the tension that seemed to have settled in permanently, and walked out of the bar. A few deep breaths of night air cleared the smoke from his lungs, but didn't do anything for his head. Tiredly, he climbed into the truck, fastened his seat belt and headed for home.

The clock on the dashboard read 11:21 when he pulled into the driveway. The house was dark and still. He wished he'd find a note saying that Masiela had packed up and moved on, but it was more likely she'd only gone to bed. On his couch. Wearing those little shorts that were nothing more than a nod at modesty and that tight little shirt that left nothing to the imagination.

Not that he had to imagine. He'd seen her naked before. Every inch of her. And he wasn't likely to ever forget it, even if she had. God knew, he'd tried.

He unlocked the door, opened it as quietly as he could and slipped inside. Call him paranoid, but he'd rather not end up staring down the barrel of her gun twice in one day. He paused a moment, heard nothing from the back of the house, then closed and locked the door and started upstairs.

He made it to his room without any sound from

downstairs, undressed and crawled into bed. But tired as he was, he couldn't sleep, and it was Masiela's fault. Donovan had left her in his care; he just needed to make sure everything was all right before he conked out.

He slid out of bed, avoided the creaky floorboard and went into the hall. He didn't bother with a light; he knew the house well enough to navigate it in pitch-black, and with the light from the moon and the street lamps filtering through the front windows, it was nowhere near that dark.

At the top of the stairs, he moved to the right, his hand on the railing, and took the first step down. His foot hit something solid and unyielding, and he lost his balance, pitching forward headfirst. "Son of a *bitch*," he gritted out, as he grabbed for something—rail, spindle, carpet—to catch himself, but momentum sent him sprawling all the way to the bottom of the stairs.

The crash startled Masiela out of a restless sleep. Automatically, she reached for her gun, its solid weight in her hand offering some sense of security, even while her brain struggled through the fog of sleep for answers. Where was she? What had awakened her? Then she heard a low groan, not too distant, and a familiar voice.

"Damn it, damn it, son of a—"

Decker's voice.

She threw back the covers and stepped cautiously into the hall doorway. The dim light revealed a shadow sprawled at the bottom of the stairs, ghostly pale patches scattered around him. Heat flushed her face. T-shirts, socks, boxer-briefs. She'd done laundry after dinner and left the basket with his clothes at the top of the stairs.

This was her fault.

She turned on the hall light as he struggled into a

sitting position, favoring his right arm. He scowled at the clothing around him, then picked up a pair of leopard print bikini panties. "I assume these are yours."

"I wouldn't be caught dead. So unless you've become promiscuous along with blind and hardheaded, *I* assume they're Dr. Cate's." She crouched in front of him. "Let me see your arm."

"You're *not* Cate."

She settled back on her heels. "I don't have to be a doctor to see it doesn't look right."

He glanced down, then paled and averted his gaze. A homicide detective and practically married to an E.R. doctor, and the obvious deformity in his own wrist made him queasy. Back when they were partners, she would have teased him about it. Back when he liked her. When she hadn't been responsible for any hurts he'd suffered.

"You need to go to the emergency room." Looking around the laundry, she found a pair of khaki shorts and held them out so he could slide his feet through.

He took them with his left hand. "I can dress myself."

"Okay." She returned to the kitchen, where she located a pair of jeans for herself, tucked the holstered pistol into the waistband, then stuck her feet into well-worn sneakers. When she returned to the stairs, Decker had managed to get the khakis as far as his knees. He was gritting his teeth, sweat dotting his forehead, and gripping the railing with his good hand in preparation to stand up. She hesitated. Should she offer assistance he wouldn't want, or wait to see if he could manage on his own?

With a bone-deep moan, he hauled himself to his feet and clung to the rail. All color was gone from his face now. He hardly seemed to notice as she pulled the shorts to his waist and fastened them.

"Where are your keys?"

"On the dresser. I need a shirt and shoes, too."

"Aw, come on. Dr. Cate's panties are in your laundry. Surely she's seen you without a shirt before."

When he glared at her, she slipped past and ran up the stairs. She dropped the keys in her pocket, found a pair of flip-flops on the closet floor and yanked both a T-shirt and a button-down shirt from their hangers. Catching sight of his wallet on the way out, she grabbed it, too, stuffing it in her hip pocket.

He was exactly where she'd left him, holding on to the stair railing for support. A bit of color had returned to his face. Unfortunately, it was an unflattering shade of green.

One tiny move convinced him that the T-shirt wasn't going to work, and the best they could manage with the other shirt was to slide it onto his left arm, then drape it over the other and pull the edges together.

He was looking pretty strained by the time he stuck out his hand. "Keys."

"I'm taking you."

"Like hell. You're in hiding, remember?"

"You're in no shape to drive."

"My left hand works fine."

"But you're right handed. And you've been drinking." The smell of alcohol on his breath must have registered subconsciously; only after she'd said the words did she realize they were true. "I'll stay in the truck. No one will have to see me. Dr. Cate won't have to see me."

He swayed unsteadily, his mouth fixed in a flat line, then carefully released the railing and started toward the door.

Masiela started to lock up, hesitated, then jogged to the dining room to retrieve her laptop case. Strap slung over her shoulder, she secured the door, followed him to the truck and helped him fasten his seat belt. Once she'd tucked the computer behind the seat, she climbed in, adjusted the seat and mirrors to accommodate her and backed out of the driveway.

He gave her directions in terse, clipped tones, then fell silent.

"The day I graduated from the academy, Yelina broke her wrist. Surgery, an appliance, screws, therapy—the whole thing. Our mother was off somewhere in Mexico, digging up bones, and our father was on his honeymoon with his new wife, so our grandmothers and I took care of her." She gave him a sidelong glance. "She was fifteen, and she took it much better than you."

"Bite me," he muttered.

"Everyone thinks men are so stoic, but I bet Dr. Cate would agree that women are much better patients."

This time the sidelong look was his. Did he wonder why she kept bringing up his girlfriend? She didn't want to. She'd rather forget the woman existed. It just seemed forgetting would be too easy, if she let herself—and too dangerous.

The hospital was on a quiet street on the east side of town. The building sprawled in three directions, additions built on as the town's needs grew, similar in appearance but not quite matching. She followed the signs to the emergency entrance, stopping under the portico. "You want a wheelchair?"

"My legs work fine. Park somewhere and stay out of sight."

Of course he meant out of everyone's sight, but naturally he was just a little more concerned about

Cate seeing her. Masiela gave him a flippant salute as he fumbled with the seatbelt. When its reel retracted, the metal buckle smacked his right arm, and he swore viciously.

He was twisting in the seat to reach the door handle, when suddenly the door swung open.

"AJ, I thought that was your truck. What are you doing out—" The woman standing outside looked from Decker to Masiela, then blinked. She was petite, pretty and managed to make the scrubs she wore look good.

She wasn't what Masiela had imagined for an exalted Calloway. Her pale brown hair was pulled straight back into a ponytail, and she wore little, if any, makeup. Her nails were short, unpolished, and the only jewelry she had on was a simple watch.

After an awkward moment, Cate refocused on AJ and his injury. "Wow. A broken wrist. I keep telling you, you should let the professionals fix up the house. I've been expecting to see you in my E.R. ever since you started." Her gaze shifted once more to Masiela. "Can you help me get him inside before you park? We're shorthanded tonight."

"I don't need help," AJ said, the instant before Masiela agreed. She surreptitiously unclipped the holster and slid it beneath the seat before she shut off the engine and climbed out. By the time she got around the truck, AJ had slid to his feet and was looking distinctly green again.

The doctor walked on his right side, Masiela on his left. Cate touched his arm naturally, as if she had the right. Masiela kept her hands at her sides, ready to grab if he needed the support.

"We'll put him in 3," Cate told the secretary as they

passed the desk. "Tell X-ray I'm sending down a right wrist in a few minutes."

Once they reached the small cubicle and AJ sat on the bed, Cate offered Masiela her hand. "I'm Cate Calloway."

Masiela eyed her hand a moment before shaking it. "I'm Luisa Gonsalves, AJ's cousin. He probably never mentioned that his uncle Mark married into a Cuban-Mexican family, did he?"

On the bed AJ scowled. She'd never worked under-cover with him, but apparently he remembered the name she'd favored. Or maybe it was how easily she lied that annoyed him. Or her making herself a member of his family.

"No, he didn't mention it." Cate looked her over, making Masiela wish she'd pulled a shirt on over the thin tank top she'd been sleeping in. "Do you live around here?"

"South Florida," Masiela said breezily. "Visiting family on my way to Atlanta."

The sound that came from AJ sounded suspiciously like a growl. "Hey, remember me? Can you do something about my arm?"

Cate rolled her gaze upward. "Men. They're such babies."

"I'll move the truck out of the entrance." Masiela lifted the curtain that closed off the cubicle and ducked out. The secretary watched curiously as she passed the desk, as did an older man reading in the waiting room.

Masiela drove the truck to the nearest parking space, then secured her weapon in the glove compartment. Decker would be happier if she waited outside, but now that Cate had seen her, what was the harm in going back in? It wasn't as if the secretary or the white-haired man could possibly recognize her. They'd noticed her only because she was a stranger, and they would forget her a few seconds after she left.

Taking deep breaths of fresh night air, she crossed the parking lot and returned inside. After just a few days of hiding, it felt so wonderful to be moving about again. She wasn't made for extended protective custody. Driving a vehicle, walking by herself, even if it was just a few hundred feet, she felt so free.

And safe. No way her enemies would connect her to Copper Lake.

She strode past the desk and back into Room 3 before stopping abruptly. The bed was empty, Decker was gone, and Cate stood at the counter, making notes in a file. Okay, so *there* was the harm in coming back inside. Time alone with Decker's girlfriend. Meeting her had been one thing. Chatting with her…

"Is AJ in X-ray?"

Cate slipped the ink pen into the pocket of her lab coat, then faced her. "Yeah. It's definitely broken. Maybe dislocated a bit. But we can take care of that. Are you staying with him?"

Who was asking? Care-giving doctor or suspicious girlfriend? Masiela smiled. "Either that or drive back to Aunt Carol Ann's."

Cate studied her a moment before nodding once, as if something she'd seen satisfied her. In a good way or bad? Masiela wondered.

"It'd be best for AJ if someone's at the house. He's going to have a little trouble managing things for a few days. I'm sure Carol Ann will be over to check on him once she hears, but I'm also sure he won't tell her tonight. How did he fall?"

Had she already asked that question of Decker?

Was she comparing stories? "I don't know. I was in the kitchen, getting a beer, and he'd gone to check on something. Next thing I heard was a crash, followed by a string of curses, and I found him stretched out on the floor." There, that was simple enough. Some truth, without too many details to trip on.

"He does like to swear when he's upset," Cate said, with a faint smile.

"He started young, and his mother was never able to break him of the habit."

"There are worse habits to pick up." Cate shifted one hip against the counter. "What do you think of the house?"

"It's great." Masiela hesitated, then plunged ahead. "Did you help him pick it out?"

"No. First I heard of it, he'd already signed the papers."

Odd. He was considering marrying the woman, and he didn't discuss the purchase of a *house* with her until it was a done deal?

"The place isn't set up yet for guests," Cate went on. "Though I guess family—" she gave Masiela another long look "—don't really count as guests, do they? And the sofa bed is comfortable enough."

"I'm a sound sleeper. It doesn't matter much where I lie down, just that I do." Discomfort itched along Masiela's spine. Cate was…doubting her? Testing her? Or just letting her know that she had a claim on Decker?

Before the doctor could respond, the curtain swished open and a young man pushed a wheelchair into the cubicle. Decker, flushed and sweaty, moved carefully from the chair to the bed, leaned back and closed his eyes.

A bit of sympathy rose inside Masiela. She hadn't

been entirely truthful when talking about Yelina's broken wrist. Her sister had passed out while the X-rays were being taken. Maneuvering broken bones into awkward positions had been more than she could bear.

Cate excused herself to go look at the X-rays, and Decker opened his eyes just enough to glare at Masiela. "Cousin?"

Moving closer to the bed, she smiled and softly asked, "Would you prefer that I'd said ex-partner? Ex-friend? One-night stand?"

The last words surprised her. They surprised him, too—and not, judging from his scowl, in a pleasant way.

Gratitude flushed through her when Cate returned, holding the curtain back in invitation. "Do you mind stepping out, Luisa? We're going to sedate him, reduce this fracture and get him into a splint."

"Sedation," Masiela repeated as she moved toward the door. "Your little cousin Yelina didn't need sedation when they reduced *her* fracture." Smiling wickedly, she ducked around the curtain and out of sight.

Chapter 7

AJ was groggy when he awoke. For one good moment, he thought he'd fallen asleep in his own bed with the lights and television still on. Then he moved, and his memory cleared fast. Going downstairs in the dark to check on Masiela. Tripping over the damn laundry basket she'd left at the top of the stairs. Falling. Breaking his wrist. Cate pulling open the door of his truck, looking from him to Masiela and back again.

His right arm was encased in a splint that extended past his elbow, and it hurt like the devil. It wasn't the only pain, either. There was a throb in his left shoulder, another in his right knee and a steady pounding in his skull. Tumbling down a flight of stairs wasn't easy on the body.

"Hey."

A soft hand touched him, and he opened his eyes to find Cate beside the bed. She looked more tired than she had when they'd come in, and there was something in her eyes.

"As soon as you feel like getting up, you can go home."

Just the thought of moving sent aches from head to toe. Still, he managed a nod.

"I've given Luisa the follow-up instructions and a prescription for pain medicine. You've got a 9:00 a.m. appointment with Dr. Stafford tomorrow. He'll x-ray you, probably put you in a cast."

He nodded again. Stafford was an orthopedic surgeon, based in Augusta, who saw patients a couple days a week in Copper Lake.

"Keep your arm elevated, ice it for fifteen to twenty minutes three or four times a day and avoid anything that causes discomfort." She started to turn away, then stopped. "She's not your cousin, is she?"

His stomach knotted. How easy would it be to lie? Just like Masiela, he'd had plenty of occasions on the job where lying wasn't just advisable but required. He could do it and do it well. But that was work. He tried not to carry it over into his personal life. "No. But I can explain."

Her smile was slight. "I don't need an explanation." Then she slid her fingers down his arm to clasp his left hand. "Actually, just meeting her explains a lot."

Made wary by her tone, he cautiously asked, "Like what?"

"Like why you go through the motions without feeling the right feelings. You think I haven't known for a while that you're not as, um, engaged in this relationship as I am?" Another faint smile at the play on words. "I've always suspected that there was someone in your past.

Someone you weren't quite over. But as long as she stayed in the past, I didn't have to acknowledge her."

"No. You're wrong, Cate."

"Tell me she wasn't important to you. Tell me you didn't care a great deal about her."

He couldn't do either. Masiela *had* been important. He *had* cared about her. But… "It was a long time ago—and not in the way you think. We worked together. We were partners." *Ex-partners. Ex-friends. A one-night stand.*

She hadn't been too drunk to remember that night. She'd just chosen to pretend it didn't happen. Why?

"I've seen you with people you work with. It's a totally different vibe. There's more here."

He shook his head stubbornly. "That's just anger. Maybe a little hostility. Things didn't go so well between us when she quit the department."

She shook her head just as stubbornly. "Lie to yourself, AJ, not to me."

"Cate, I'm not—" He broke off. He wasn't lying, not about Masiela. But it was true that he didn't feel the right feelings. He liked Cate a lot. He might even love her, but not in the way he should. Not in the way he needed to marry her. Hadn't he acknowledged in the last few days that she deserved more? And if it made her feel better to think he couldn't give her that because of Masiela…

She gave his fingers a squeeze before pulling away. "I sent Luisa to get the truck. She should be at the door by now. Do you need help getting into this chair?"

Slowly he sat up, letting his legs dangle over the side of the bed. "Cate—"

She smiled. "Don't worry. I'm okay. Really."

He looked at her a long time. Was there more truth in her face than he'd expected? Sixteen years on the job had taught him how to read people, and she didn't seem as upset as he might have predicted. There was a bit of sadness in her eyes, but mostly it was resignation. Acceptance. She looked like someone whose casual relationship had just ended, not like a woman who'd just found out that the man she loved didn't love her back. She didn't even look close to heartbroken.

Maybe there was someone in *her* past that she hadn't yet gotten over.

Cate waited next to the wheelchair, ready to help. He stood, gritting his teeth, then carefully lowered himself into the chair. She flipped the footrests into place, unlocked the brakes and pushed him from the cubicle.

His truck was parked underneath the portico again, and Masiela waited beside the open passenger door. He should have made her stay home, shouldn't have taken the risk of her running into Cate. But it wasn't regret that eased the tension in his shoulders, just relief that things were ended with Cate.

He worked his way into the seat, stifling a sharp intake of breath at the pain the effort caused. This time it was Cate leaning across to fasten the seat belt, smelling of crisp cotton and shampoo.

"You got everything?" she asked, and Masiela nodded. With a nod of her own, Cate stepped back. "No work until you see Dr. Stafford. Take care of him, Luisa." Then she grinned, and he recognized clearly what she was feeling: relief, just like him.

Maybe, like him, she thought it was time to settle down and have kids. Maybe, like him, she thought he was as acceptable a candidate as anyone. Apparently, like him, she hadn't really been in love.

After she closed the door, Masiela shifted into gear and drove away. They were halfway to Copper Lake's only all-night pharmacy before she broke her silence. "She's nice."

"Yeah."

Another block passed. "Did she buy my story?"

"No."

One more block. "Sorry."

"Don't be. She's not." He waited until she'd turned into the drive-through before grudgingly adding, "I'm not."

She had nothing to say to that.

A drowsy-looking clerk sent the pain medication out through the tube, and Masiela pulled away from the drive-through and stopped in the parking lot before twisting open the bottle and shaking out two tablets. Clutching them in one hand, she opened the bottle of water she'd bought earlier from a waiting room vending machine, then offered both to Decker. "Take these."

His heavy-lidded gaze shifted from one hand to the other. "I can wait until we're home."

"You can, but there's no reason. It takes them a while to kick in. You'll be tucked in your bed before you get any goofier than you already are. Take them."

It was a testament to the severity of his pain that he obeyed without further argument. After washing down the pills, he laid his head back and closed his eyes with a sigh that sounded a lot more like a groan.

Suddenly she was tired, too, more than the late hour could justify. Wishing she'd paid more attention to the directions he'd given her, she turned onto the first westbound street she came to. The worst that could happen, she would have to find her way downtown and start again from there. Luck was with her, though. She found Oglethorpe and turned onto it, only two blocks from their destination.

She slowed, about to pull in the driveway, when movement in the house caught her eye. Through the uncurtained front windows she saw a form pass from left to right, then a second appeared in the hallway. She glanced at Decker, his chin dipped to his chest, and grimaced. Clearly, she'd underestimated the power of the pain pills mixed with whatever medication he'd been given at the hospital.

Easing her foot off the brake, she drove slowly on. Lights were off in most of the neighboring houses, and the only two cars parked on the street both had Georgia tags. Of course, any intruder with half a brain would leave his vehicle elsewhere and hike in through the woods behind the house.

Half a block away, houses gave way to woods on her side of the road. She eased the truck into the shadows of a huge tree and retrieved her pistol from the glove box. "Decker?"

A quiet snore was his only response.

Her fingers were knotted, her stomach cramping, as she studied her options. She could get the hell out, find a motel a town or two over for them to spend the night, and let him deal with it all in the morning. She could make an anonymous call to the police department, but if they went in expecting vandals or burglars and found killer cops instead...

Or she could walk back through the woods and try to catch a glimpse of the intruders herself. To confirm that it was an eighteen-year-old punk and his buddy, obnoxious but not much of a danger, or something— someone—far worse.

You don't go out. You stay out of sight.

I'm not stupid, Decker, she'd told him the first time. *I understand the concept of hiding out.*

Was sneaking around in the dark stupid? Sure, if she wasn't armed. If she didn't have the benefit of being as well trained as the bad cops and way better prepared for trouble than a couple of teenage punks. Besides, she wasn't going to confront anyone. They'd never know she was there.

And she *needed* to know if she'd been found. If she'd brought danger to Decker's door.

She pocketed the keys, then slid to the ground, pushing the door closed with as little noise as possible. After attaching the holster to her waistband, she withdrew the pistol, keeping it at her side as she moved deeper into the trees. The night was quiet: she heard a truck braking on a road nearby, an owl hooting closer. It was entirely too peaceful a setting for danger…which made the possible threat that much scarier. She expected goose bumps and knotted nerves when she was walking into a dimly lit tenement where violence was the norm, but not in woods surrounded by houses filled with sleeping residents, not with a bright moon overhead and a lazy breeze drifting the scent of summer flowers on the air.

Masiela circled behind the house north of Decker's and crouched in the shadows of its fence near the edge of the trees. Decker's back door stood open, casting a wedge of pale light onto the grass. Voices sounded distant: male, at least two, possibly three, making no effort to be covert.

She judged the distance between her hiding spot and Decker's house. If she got close enough to hear the voices clearly, to make out what they were saying, she'd have her answer. The Brat Packs' voices were burned into her memory—every insult, every innuendo, every threat.

Forty feet to the side of the house, ten more to the back stoop. If the intruders talked on their way out, she would have enough warning to make it back around the side of the house. If they surprised her in the open with no cover…

Snuffling immediately to her left startled her, and she had to shove out her right hand to stop herself from tumbling over. On the other side of the board fence, sniffing switched to a low whine that quickly ramped up into barking.

"Shh! Good dog," she whispered. "Be quiet, puppy."

The dog continued to bark, his paws scrabbling in the dirt. Masiela shushed him again, then put a few feet's distance between them. Her action excited the animal further, his barks turning to rapid, squealing yips.

A shadow, tall and distorted, fell across the patch of light spilling from the door. "Hey," the form called. "Let's get out before that mutt wakes everyone up."

By now the dog was hysterical, making Masiela's ears ring. She ducked behind the nearest tree, staring at the figure in the doorway. Backlit as he was, it was impossible to tell anything about him except that he was tall and muscular. That matched both Kinney and Taylor, though she figured a star pitcher might fit the description, too.

She held her breath, willing the dog to shut up and the guys in the house to come out where she could see them. When the barking went silent for a moment, she thought the first wish had been granted, until another voice cut through the night.

"Pepper, we're trying to sleep in here. What's gotten into you?"

The dog went into a frenzy, racing around the yard, then circling back to the fence, making as much noise as a dozen sugar-fueled kids. Swearing silently, Masiela watched the intruder take a step back, out of sight, then surged to her feet and ran the opposite direction. The unseen Pepper followed her progress along the fence, with her disgruntled master muttering, "What the hell?" an instant before the backyard lights blazed on.

Keeping a firm grip on her pistol, Masiela sprinted forward, her gaze locked on the ground ahead and any obstacles that might trip her. She didn't slow until she reached the truck, where Decker still snoozed, and she didn't manage a full breath until they were parked in the back corner of the parking lot of an all-night convenience store two miles away.

Thanks to the damn dog, she couldn't say whether the one voice she'd really heard belonged to one of her enemies; and seeing him—a dark shape wearing dark clothes, with his face obscured by shadows—had been useless. Admittedly, partly her fault.

Kind of like her protector's condition at the moment. She gazed at Decker with a thin smile. She could wake him if she tried hard enough, but she knew from experience that he'd be groggy and thickheaded. He didn't handle narcotics well; they either made him loopy or knocked him out, nothing in between.

Okay, so her plan had failed. Next step: call the police? It was the obvious action, one she would have taken without hesitation, until the past few months. Now everything inside her protested. If anyone from Decker's department had to know she was there, let him choose the person, the one he could absolutely trust, the way he trusted the Brat Pack. The way he'd once trusted *her*.

She yawned so wide that her jaw popped, leading to her decision: they both needed rest—someplace safe, someplace other than Copper Lake. She used the truck's onboard navigation system to choose a town seventeen miles away and a motel on its far side.

It was an easy drive on a moonlit road with little traffic. She found the motel, parked out of sight of the office and checked in with cash she'd stowed in her laptop case before leaving Dallas. Key card in hand, Masiela returned to the truck and opened the passenger door. "Decker." She gave his leg a shake. "Hey, Decker, come on, wake up. Time to go to bed."

He opened his eyes, nodded and murmured, "I'm okay here."

She cajoled, commanded and pestered until she finally got him inside, out of the awkwardly hanging shirt and onto the closest bed. A few seconds later, he was snoring again. The other bed looked damned appealing, but not yet. Tucking the key card in her pocket, she climbed into the truck and drove a few blocks away, parking it in the lot of an apartment complex, unnoticeable among all the other vehicles. Then, laptop tucked to her side and pistol in easy reach in its holster, she jogged back to the motel, let herself in, locked up and leaned against the door with a heavy sigh.

Masiela took the time to gently prop two of the room's four pillows under Decker's right arm, then turned on the bathroom light before sinking onto the second bed and immediately dozing off. It seemed like only minutes later when a string of curses woke her.

Decker was sitting up on the edge of the bed, cradling his arm to his chest, groggy, pain etching deep lines in his face. "What the hell—? Where the hell—?" His gaze shot to her as she sat up, and he demanded, "What the hell's going on? Where are we? What happened?"

Shoving her hair from her face, she forced her eyes to focus on the nightstand clock. She'd slept three hours, which meant his next dose of pain medication was past due. "Give me a minute," she mumbled, rising from the bed and heading for the bathroom sink. She splashed water on her face, dried it, filled a paper cup and returned to the beds with it and the pain pills. "We're in a motel in Peachton. You remember going to the emergency room?"

He grunted. "We were supposed to go home from there."

"We did. But somebody else was already there. At least two males. Went in the back door. I couldn't get a good look at either one, and thanks to the furball next door, I couldn't hear the one guy's voice well enough to recognize it."

Stillness settled over him, his arm apparently forgotten. "You went in to check it out?"

That was a voice she remembered well, cold and menacing, usually followed by an angry eruption that led to a lot of shouting. She tried to head it off with reason. "You were passed out, unarmed and incapacitated. I wasn't about to call the police, and I needed to find out what I could before I went running off to hide. I was armed and I was careful."

He took a slow breath. "Not careful enough to outwit Pepper."

Masiela blinked. "I got caught by a dog named Pepper?"

"Yeah. She's about as big as your shoe." Another slow breath.

Interesting. She was way more familiar with Decker in a temper than she was with him trying to control it.

"So what did you find out?"

She grimaced. "Not much. I saw two figures inside,

then one at the back door. He was tall, muscular and every other detail was in shadow."

"You didn't recognize him."

She shook her head and waited for him to say something snide: *You didn't recognize him because it wasn't Myers, Kinney or Taylor, because they're not after you, because they had nothing to do with Teri's murder, because your client is guilty.* When he didn't, she drew a breath to ease the tightness in her muscles, then asked, "How do you feel?"

This time he grimaced. "Like I fell down a flight of stairs and broke my damn wrist."

She wasn't about to give voice to the twinge of sympathy deep down inside. In her experience, the more sympathy men got, the more they wanted, and pampering wasn't her style. "Poor baby. Here are your pills." She took two from the bottle.

"I just want one."

"Okay. Here's one pill." She handed it to him, then the water, waited until he swallowed, then held out the second tablet. "Here's the other one."

"I don't need two."

"Are you hurting?"

Even in the dim light she could make out his glare. "Like hell."

"Then take the second pill. It's easier to keep the pain under control than to chase it when it's out of control."

He stared at the pill but made no move to take it. She made no move to withdraw it. After a long moment ticked past, he grudgingly accepted it and swallowed it with a gulp of water.

"Still no better at being the patient, are you? That time you sprained your ankle chasing a suspect, we thought

we were going to have to put you down like a horse
gone lame."

"I damn near broke it," he growled.

"Yeah, so you kept telling us. It might even have hurt
as much as my face did when that three-hundred-pound
gorilla punched me, but you didn't hear me complain,
did you?" Now things would be different, but that had
been in her better-than days: she'd had to be better than
the male officers she worked with to be considered half
as good. She would have bitten off her tongue before
complaining to any of them about the pain—or the fact
that her backup hadn't backed her up.

"Yeah, well, you didn't have to bear weight on your
face."

"No, I just had to eat, breathe and talk."

Silence settled between them, heavy, thick, the kind
where sounds magnified in her ears. When it grew so
loud she was tempted to plug her ears with her fingers,
he broke it.

"Why didn't you tell me?"

He'd asked the question earlier that evening, along
with others, and she'd buried her answer in the answer
to the others. *You know how narrow-minded cops are
when it comes to their own.* How narrow-minded *he* was
when it came to his own.

She'd been one of "their own," too, but there wouldn't
have been any sympathy or support for her. It was always
the cops being accused who got the backing of their
fellow officers. In an us against them environment, the
cop doing the accusing suddenly became one of "them,"
the enemy.

"You don't believe me now. Why pretend that you
might have all those years ago?" Even though they'd been
best buds and partners and had trusted each other with

their lives, he would have said she was overly sensitive or reacting out of her dislike for the three cops. They'd never been out of line when anyone else was around, so it would have come down to her word against theirs. And Decker would have believed them.

"I never saw anything inappropriate."

She snorted. "They're corrupt, not stupid. They were careful. They didn't do anything in front of witnesses."

"And yet Kinney left that message on your answering machine."

"Yeah, well, he must have felt safe, don't you think? After all, he'd gotten away with murder."

Silence again, filled with tension that was echoed in his voice when he finally spoke. "If I believed for one second that they killed Teri—"

And she snorted again. "You don't want to believe. You made a rookie mistake, Decker. You settled for the obvious answer. You didn't look at the evidence. You didn't care if it was all just a little too neat. You knew Rodriguez had killed one of his girls when she tried to leave him, you knew Teri intended to leave him and you assumed he killed her, too. But you were wrong."

He leaned forward, his hazel gaze locking with hers. "You and I were partners. We shared everything. And you expect me to believe that all this crap was going on between you and the others but you kept it to yourself… until now, when you're trying to destroy their careers. You were a good cop, Mas. Tell me that's not damned convenient."

Too antsy to remain still, she sprang up from the bed and paced to the window, lifting the heavy drape just enough to see out. What Decker had said happened often enough: someone was arrested for rape or assault or robbery, and after his picture appeared in the media, suddenly, people who had never filed a report came forward, saying, "Oh, he did the same thing to me." Sometimes they told the truth. Sometimes they didn't.

If their situations were reversed, if he were accusing three officers of murder and suddenly revealed wrongdoing on their part from years ago, would she think it was awfully convenient that he felt moved to share the information now?

Anyone but Decker, and her answer would likely be yes. But she'd always trusted him implicitly. If he'd told her that the sun was now rising in the west, she would have nodded and turned her chair 180 degrees for the best view.

But she hadn't believed him when he insisted that the Brat Pack hadn't killed Teri, because she knew things he didn't. She'd seen a side to the men he hadn't.

"Come on, counselor," Decker said. "You were always quick with the glib words and double-talk. Give me an answer."

She stared out the window a moment longer before slowly facing him. "You don't need answers from me, Decker. You think you've already got them all. Someday, maybe you'll find the nerve to look at what I've found. Until then, talking is pointless. You should lie down and try to get some sleep. That's what I'm going to do."

Without letting herself look at him, she returned to the far bed, threw back the covers, kicked off her shoes and lay down. Thankfully, not long after her head hit the pillow, she slept.

Chapter 8

Thursday morning, AJ awoke to the steady throb of pain. He was stiff and sore, his entire right arm hurt like the devil and his headache had achieved major proportions. If he thought he could go back to sleep, he'd give it a shot, but since he doubted that was going to happen, not when he was hurting like this, he shifted enough to see the clock—7:00 a.m.—and pulled the phone as far as it would go.

Maricci sounded too damn cheery when he answered his cell. Of course, he hadn't fallen down the stairs and broken his damn wrist and didn't have Masiela to deal with.

AJ filled him in: the fall, the E.R., the intruders in his house, the motel. He left enough out to make any good detective curious, but Maricci didn't ask for more information. Instead, his response was simple. "What do you need?"

AJ's gaze strayed to the other bed, where Masiela lay, her breathing steady, her back to him, that silky black hair vivid against the cheap, white linens. What he really needed was to get her out of his care, out of his life. But he'd given Donovan his word, and he couldn't go back on that. Wouldn't, even if he could. "A ride to Copper Lake. And bring someone with you. Ty. He'll need to stay here while we're gone."

"We'll be there soon."

With a grunt, AJ hung up, then cautiously got to his feet. After an awkward visit to the bathroom, he looked at himself in the mirror and winced. The splint made his arm appear twice its size, his fingers extending beyond it were purplish-red, a large bruise blackened his right knee, and another stretched along his left shoulder. In sixteen years as a cop, he'd looked worse before. He couldn't remember feeling worse, though. Even the simple act of his heart beating made his wrist hurt.

"There's a diner across the street," Masiela called. "I ordered breakfast and offered them a ten-dollar tip to deliver it."

His first thought was to tell her all he wanted was pain pills, but the growl in his stomach disagreed. "Thanks."

By the time he'd struggled into his shirt, a knock sounded at the door. He limped across the room, where Masiela waited behind the door, gun in hand. She gave him a twenty, then undid the locks so he could open the door.

A gum-chewing waitress gave him a bag of food and a cardboard carrier with coffee, took the money and said a pleasant "Thanks" before she left.

As she prepared her own food, he watched her, wondering what was going on behind those weary brown eyes. God knew, her mind was a strange and mysterious place, where it made sense to switch from being a good cop to a scum-representing lawyer. Where she preferred to pretend nothing had happened, rather than acknowledge that she'd had sex with her partner.

The reminder that she knew about that night made his jaw clench. He washed down a bite of burrito, then fixed a stare on her. "Just how drunk were you that night?"

She didn't pretend she didn't know what he was talking about, but she took her time answering, thoroughly chewing her food, swallowing, wiping her mouth with a napkin. "Not as drunk as you apparently thought I was."

"Why didn't you ever say anything?"

"Why didn't *you?*" she shot back.

Part of him hadn't wanted to acknowledge it. They'd had such a good working relationship—and any idiot knew that getting personal was the best way to royally screw that up.

But the part of him that did want to acknowledge it had been waiting for her to do so first—to at least give some hint that she knew what they'd done—that part had been bothered that she apparently had no memory of what had been a few damn good hours in his life. What man wanted to think he was that forgettable?

"I thought you didn't remember…"

"So you acted like you didn't?" She snorted.

He'd awakened that morning before dawn, feeling pretty good despite the fact he'd had only a few hours' sleep—at least, for the first couple minutes. Then the impact of what they'd done hit him: him and Mas, down and dirty and naked. All he could think was that he'd screwed up, that he'd risked the best partnership he'd ever had…and he wasn't sure he regretted it.

Not sure what to think—or to want—he'd left her apartment while she still slept. He'd run eight miles, showered and been at his desk when she walked into work. No one would have guessed to look at her that she'd had too much to drink the night before or that anything had changed between her and AJ. AJ *knew* what had happened, and he couldn't see even the faintest hint of it in her face or her actions. The way she looked at him, her tone of voice, her behavior—nothing was different from before.

And so he'd done his damnedest to act the same.

She finished eating her breakfast and sat, coffee cup cradled in both hands, watching him, unsatisfied with his last response. He shrugged awkwardly. "Since you didn't say anything, I figured it would be best to ignore it."

"If *you* had said something, I would have responded." She snorted again. "Don't forget, *you* were the one who sneaked out while I was asleep."

His first impulse was to dispute her characterization; he had simply left. He'd had things to do before work. But he could have spared the time to wake her and tell her goodbye. He could have left a note for her. He could have invited her to run the eight miles with him. They'd done it plenty of times before. Instead he had very quietly gathered his clothes, gotten dressed in the darkened living room and left.

Wasn't that pretty much the definition of sneaking out?

Heat flushed his face. "I'd never slept with anyone I worked with," he mumbled.

"Neither had I."

"It was stupid."

"I agree."

Her expression was cool, her tone even. He studied her, wondering where his people-reading skills had disappeared to, because he couldn't ID a single damn emotion on her face or in her voice.

"But I don't regret it," he said belligerently, and there was a flash: surprise. For a moment she was at a loss for words. He sat there, scowling, waiting for her to recover.

Waiting to hear that she regretted it.

Or not.

After a while, she took a breath and opened her mouth…and a knock sounded at the door. Obviously considering the interruption a reprieve, she clamped her jaw shut again.

He glanced toward the door. "My best detectives."

"How much did you tell them?"

"Not enough that they'll be expecting you," he said drily.

Another knock came, followed by a low-pitched voice. "Hey, AJ, it's us."

Masiela crossed the room, undoing the locks, then stepping back into the shadows as she opened the door. Maricci was first through, followed by Ty Gadney. When she moved to close and lock the door behind them, both men looked at her, at the pistol she wore, then at AJ. Maricci didn't look surprised; he never did. The emotion flickered through Ty's gaze, then he schooled his expression to a good imitation of Maricci's cool blankness.

Decker turned on the bedside lamp and, following his lead, Masiela hit the overhead light. "Masiela Leal, Tommy Maricci and Ty Gadney."

The three exchanged nods before she returned to sit

on the other bed and pick up her coffee. She didn't sip it, though. Just used it to hold on to.

"We went by your house on the way here," Maricci said. "Russ is fixing the back door and the light now, so the place will be secure, then you and I can go by for a look around after you see the doctor."

"Thanks." AJ paused before bluntly saying, "Mas ran into some trouble back home. There's a chance it might have followed her here. Ty, I need you to stay here with Mas."

Ty nodded somberly. "Anything in particular we should be watching for, here or at home?"

"Anyone who doesn't belong. Anyone who might be asking questions about Mas or me. Anyone from Texas." Decker hesitated, then forced the final words out. "Particularly the Dallas PD."

The change in both men was palpable: sudden stillness, the immediate understanding that the people after Masiela were, like them, cops. It said a hell of a lot for their working relationship that they didn't ask questions, voice concerns or even ask if she was wanted elsewhere. They both simply nodded.

AJ stood up, biting back a groan, and gestured to his shirt. "Can you…?"

Masiela set aside the coffee and did up the rest of the buttons. She stood close enough that he could smell the faded fragrance clinging to her skin and hair. He recognized it from his bathroom, where his shaving cream and bath soap had been pushed to the side by an entire array of her stuff, all in this same sweet fragrance.

Done, she held out the pill bottle. "Take some of these."

He shook his head. "If I hadn't taken them last night, I might have been of more use."

"If you hadn't taken them, you would have been in too much pain to be of any use."

"You know how I get with narcotics." He thought she might try to out-stubborn him, but after a moment, she nodded and set the bottle down again.

"Be careful," he told both her and Ty as he picked up his keys from the table, then limped to the door with Maricci following.

Both gave the same answer: "I always am."

When the door closed, Gadney secured the locks while Masiela gathered the trash from breakfast and dropped it into the can under the sink. That done, she straightened first her bed, then Decker's, before sitting down on it. "You might as well make yourself comfortable, detective."

"Call me Ty," he said politely as he took a seat on her bed.

Maricci was tall, dark and gorgeous. Ty was also tall, though leaner, darker and also gorgeous. A black detective in a small Southern town. She'd bet they had more than a few experiences in common.

"You didn't ask Decker many questions."

"Didn't need to. He's the lieutenant." His expression turned thoughtful, then he amended that. "He's AJ."

Not blind obedience to his boss, but loyalty to the man. Mas knew the feeling well. She just wished it had been reciprocated.

"You been with the department long?" Without the neat beard that hugged his jaw, she would guess he was about twenty years old and far too wide-eyed to be a detective. Obviously, she would be wrong.

"Seven years. Been a detective five weeks." His grin was quick and devastating. "You don't advance real quick in Copper Lake. People get in the job and stay until retirement."

"Is that your plan?"

"Yeah. It wasn't yours?"

Masiela smiled faintly. "You think I was a cop?"

"I'm thinking not a lot of people outside of cops are as comfortable wearing a gun as you are."

"Dallas PD. I worked to put myself through law school, then became a defense attorney."

"Bet that went over big with the guys you worked with."

"Yeah, not so much." She drew her feet onto the bed and leaned against the pillows that smelled of Decker. In all the years she'd known him, he hadn't switched colognes. He'd found one that worked for him—earthy, rich, sexy—and stuck with it. Sometimes, when she was weak, it had haunted her. Now it just smelled comfortable. Familiar. Safe.

With another sweet breath, she laid the situation out for Gadney. "I don't have any warrants outstanding. I've never been arrested. But I have been threatened, and the guys who did it are homicide detectives. They've killed before, and there's no reason to think they won't do it again. Decker's not convinced they're guilty, but he agreed to give me a safe place to lay low."

"Which turned out to be not so safe. Is there any way you can find out if your guys are still in Dallas?"

She considered it. Like any good ADA, Donovan had sources within the police department. Finding out if three officers had been on the job the day before would be a simple matter. Getting a hold of phone records for the district attorney's office, for the Brat Pack, wouldn't.

Retrieving her laptop case, she took a notepad from the zippered pocket. "Use your cell phone and dial this number." She read it off, then returned the pad to the case. "His name is Ray Donovan. Give the secretary your first name and tell her you're an old friend of his from Georgia. Don't leave a message if he's out."

Ty's voice was friendly, charming with its soft Southern flow when the call was answered. "Hey, is my man Ray in?" A pause. "Yeah, I know, he's always busy. That's the life of a hotshot prosecutor. But I'm sure he'll take a couple minutes for me. Tell him it's Tyler, his old buddy from Georgia."

After a moment, he held out the phone, and she took it. Her palm was clammy, her muscles taut. "Donovan."

His tone took on a strained note. Not only was she not the buddy he was expecting, he'd probably figured she would be the last person to call him. "What's up?"

"We had visitors last night. At least two, could have been three. Can you find out if everyone showed up for work last night?" The three detectives worked shift three. If they'd been on the job until midnight, there was no way they could have made it to Georgia in time to break into Decker's house.

"I'll find out. Why are you calling instead of my 'old buddy'?"

She smiled tightly again. "He's getting a cast put on his wrist. Long story. Let us know, will you?" Ending the call, she gave the phone back to Ty, then settled back against the pillows, catching a faint whiff of Decker's cologne again.

"Even if they were at work, it doesn't mean they couldn't have hired someone," Ty pointed out.

"Yeah. But these guys...we go back a long way. It's

personal. I don't think they would give someone else the pleasure of dealing with me."

"So now what? We wait?"

"Yeah." She stifled a sigh. "Now we wait."

As they approached the Copper Lake city limits, Maricci finally turned the conversation to what was apparently on his mind—what had been on AJ's mind since they'd left the motel. "So…you two used to… what?"

"She was a cop. We were partners."

"Hmm. I would've guessed…"

What? That there was more? AJ had always been satisfied with *partners* to describe what was between him and Mas, but looking back, it seemed inadequate. She'd been his best friend, the key important person in his life, the one he'd trusted more than any other—except when it had mattered the most: when her doubts about Kinney and the others had threatened his ideas of honor and friendship. He had been persuaded—by others and himself—that it was one pissed-off ex-cop trying to undermine the reputations of three good cops.

And that had been grossly unfair. It hadn't been a pissed-off ex-cop making accusations; it was *Masiela,* his partner, best friend, the most important person in his life. He'd owed her a hell of a lot more than he'd given.

"Anything you want to share about her trouble?" Maricci asked as he pulled into the parking lot that served various doctors' offices.

AJ had brought him and Gadney into this. They deserved to know what they might be up against. "She's got the DA's office—Donovan, the guy you met the other day—looking into an old case, her first homicide as a lawyer. Guy was convicted and sentenced to life. She thinks the cops on the case may have…"

"Framed him?" Maricci supplied when he didn't finish.

"May have committed the murder themselves." It was hard to say. AJ could talk about corruption in police departments, but when it came to cops he knew—and when the victim was someone he'd felt responsible for—it was tough to wrap his mind around.

With the emotional distance of uninvolvement, Maricci shrugged. "You know that shit happens."

"You ever work with a dirty cop?"

"Not that I know of. Some lazy ones. Incompetent. One who questioned a suspect without Mirandizing her, then suggested we could testify that she wasn't a suspect at the time. But that was more inexperience and overenthusiasm than corruption."

Maricci stopped in front of the brick building that housed Dr. Stafford's clinic, and AJ clumsily unfastened his seat belt. Before opening the door, though, he grimly said, "I knew these guys since the first day at the academy. One of them saved my life when we worked narcotics. It's just hard to believe…"

"Everyone has secrets, Lieutenant."

After a moment, Maricci shrugged again. "While you're here, I'm going back to your house to look around. Call me when you're done."

AJ nodded as he climbed out of the car and went inside. When the nurse called him after an hour-long wait, she first took him to X-ray for more films that left him sweating and nauseous, then to an exam room.

Stafford came in as the nurse removed the splint and unwrapped layers of cotton to expose AJ's bruised, swollen wrist. "Falling down the stairs, Lieutenant.

Seems a cop could find more exciting ways to get hurt,"
Stafford remarked with a grin.

"Next time I'll try to get shot."

"Nah, bullets do nasty things when they go through
bone. The X-rays show that your wrist is in good position,
so we'll get you fixed up with a cast, then see you back
in four weeks."

"What about work?"

"Once you can get through the day with only
acetaminophen or ibuprofen, then you're good to go."
Stafford paused to make a notation, then gave him a
warning look. "But don't go without the narcotics when
you really need them, just so you can work. The job's
not going anywhere."

That damn sure was true, AJ reflected as he walked
out fifteen minutes later, sporting a black cast from the
base of his fingers to just below his elbow, along with a
sling that was already cutting into his shoulder and neck.
As long as there were criminals, there would be cops.

And when the two happened to be one and the
same...

Just the thought made him feel as sick as he had when
the X-ray tech had been twisting his arm in there.

Maricci was waiting in the parking lot. AJ settled in
the passenger seat, then propped his right wrist on his
left shoulder, taking the pressure off the sling strap and
hoping it would ease the throbbing. He hurt so bad that
he wanted to lean over and puke, but the effort might
make him pass out. Besides, Maricci was fastidious
about his car. He'd reamed Kiki for tossing a candy bar
wrapper in the back when they were on surveillance one
time, and AJ had to listen to her complain for two solid
days.

"Bet you wish you'd taken those pain pills your friend

was pushing, don't you?" Maricci asked. "I've seen pretty much all there is to see at the house. You wanna go back to the motel?"

A slow breath helped ease the nausea. "Nah. I've got to pick up some stuff. My cell phone…" He paused as Maricci handed it over. "My weapon. Did you find how they got in?"

"The back door was jimmied. Pretty good job of it, too. Did you move that TV that was in front of the sofa? Because it's not there now. There's clothes scattered around the stairs, but nothing else seems to be missing. Oh, and they painted a few obscenities on the Sheetrock in the living room."

AJ scowled. "Stealing a television, graffiti…doesn't sound like cops trying to shut someone up, does it?"

"Nope. More like kids that you almost arrested for stealing a television a couple days ago. Connor Calloway's family had him out of jail within two hours yesterday. That gave him the rest of the day to persuade those idiot Holigan brothers to go along with him." Maricci pulled into AJ's driveway. "I sent Isaacs over to pick up the brothers. We'll keep them waiting for an hour or two before I question them."

If the break-in turned out to be the work of vandals, Masiela would be relieved—though she wouldn't be thrilled that three pretty much harmless teenage punks had driven her even deeper into hiding. Better that she be safe, though, than AJ be sorry.

Fishing his keys out with his left hand, he went inside the house and surveyed the handiwork in the living room. Neon-colored curses marked each of the four walls, one of them misspelled. No one had ever accused the Holigans of being smart.

While Maricci secured the back door temporarily with

a two-by-four and nails, AJ took a slow walk-through that showed nothing else out of place besides the TV. The clothes basket that had caused his fall remained where it had landed, the clothing still scattered. His bedroom was undisturbed, with no noticeable attempt to get into the gun safe in his closet where he kept his pistol and badge.

He'd just taken out the pistol and two extra magazines when his cell phone rang. "Yeah," he muttered.

"Good morning to you, too," Donovan said. "Tell your house guest that I checked, and all three of our friends worked their usual shift last night. No way they could have paid you a visit."

So Masiela had called Donovan. He would have thought of that sooner or later. Probably much later, after a double dose of pain pills. "Yeah, it looks more like stupid kids. Maricci'll find out for sure."

"Be careful until then. I don't want anything happening to Masiela."

You and me both. He hesitated, then gruffly said, "I assume you've been examining her evidence. What do you think?"

"You haven't looked at it yourself yet? No, of course you haven't. You were buddies with them and pissed off at her." Another voice sounded in the background, a woman, then Donovan said, "I've got to go. My jury's just come back. I'll call you."

Israel Rodriguez might be innocent of this particular crime, Donovan had said on Monday. Masiela had been saying it for years, and AJ had been resisting it for years. What if she was right? What if he'd been ticked off at her all this time and she'd been right and he'd been wrong?

He felt sick again, and this time he couldn't blame it on pain.

Since he couldn't bring Masiela back to the house until they were positive Connor and his buds were their visitors—a confession or hard proof would be nice—he dumped some clothes, shampoo and stuff into a duffel and carried it downstairs, then pointed out Masiela's suitcase. As soon as Maricci placed both bags in the trunk, they were on their way back to Peachton.

When they were parked in front of the motel room, Maricci said, "You don't have to look so sour. She can't be too big a hardship to come home to. She looked pretty damn sexy with that gun on her hip."

There *was* something about a woman as capable and tough—and feminine and soft—as Mas, AJ admitted to himself. The problem was, it was all so damn complicated.

"She can outshoot and outrun you and me both. She could probably get the best of us in a fight, too."

"And she's beautiful. Gotta love her."

Oh, yeah, he'd loved her. Once. Her going to work as a defense lawyer and taking on Rodriguez's case had ended that. Even if Rodriguez had been innocent, someone else could have represented him. Someone else could have continued to fight for him.

Someone else could have done the right thing, a snide voice whispered.

Though it was looking more and more like AJ hadn't.

After flipping through the channels once, Masiela surrendered the TV remote to Ty, then paced to the window to gaze out through a narrow crack. What she could see of the parking lot was empty, the only movement being the housekeepers as they pushed their carts from room to room. Decker and Maricci had been gone more than two hours, and she'd spent most of the time wondering. What had the doctor said about Decker's arm? What had they found at the house? Had Donovan gotten in touch with them yet? Could they go back home soon, or were more dimly lit, musty-scented motel rooms in her future?

Home. It seemed odd that she would think of Decker's house that way, but why not? His apartment in Dallas had been home as much as her own place had. *He* had been home. At his side, working together, playing together, having his back—that was where she'd been happy. Where she'd belonged.

Until she turned down the job with the DA's office and taken Rodriguez's case.

The flash of a turn signal drew her attention to the Dodge turning into the parking lot. The tightening of her muscles would have told her it was Decker, even if she couldn't see him in the front seat. He looked exhausted, in serious pain. *Poor baby,* she thought, without a hint of the usual sarcasm.

When Maricci parked in front of the door, she moved away from the window, heading for the sink to get a cup of water. "They're back."

Ty rose from the bed and crossed to the door, checking the peephole before undoing the locks. Decker came in first, death warmed over, and went straight to his bed. By the time he was settled, she had the water and two pain pills waiting for him, and he took them without protest.

Maricci was on his cell, not saying much beyond the occasional murmur. After a few moments, he ended the conversation. "Good job, Isaacs. Thanks."

"I bet that hurt," Decker muttered, his eyes closed. "Complimenting Kiki. Thanking her."

"Hey, I compliment her when she deserves it," Maricci replied. "When she picked up the Holigans, she brought their mom in, too, since the younger one's seventeen. Mom tends bar across the river and didn't get home until four, so she wasn't real thrilled to be dragged out of bed and down to the station. She told Isaacs all about the television in the living room this morning that wasn't there when she left last night. Neither of the kids would admit that Connor was in on it, but at least we know for sure it was homegrown punks instead of out-of-state ones."

Masiela sank down on the edge of her bed. "Kids," she echoed. She was chagrined. All that fear, all that adrenaline, over nothing. Oh, sure, she'd come up against teenagers before who were stone-cold killers, but that wasn't the case with *these* kids. They were holding a grudge, looking for a thrill and too dumb to get rid of the evidence.

She was also relieved. She was still safe. Decker was still safe, except—she glanced at his cast—from her.

"So we can go home," she said hopefully.

"We'll follow you," Maricci said. "Where's the truck?"

She told him, and in a matter of minutes, he had retrieved Decker's truck and Ty had checked them out of the room. Ty helped Decker into the pickup while she and Maricci kept watch, then she climbed behind the wheel, started the powerful engine and backed out.

* * *

When she parked in Decker's driveway a half hour later, her earlier thought returned: *Home*.

But not for long.

"Thanks for everything," Masiela said, glancing over her shoulder as Decker wearily climbed the stairs. He'd be snoring before his friends made it to the edge of the porch. "Thanks for everything."

Maricci pulled a card from his hip pocket, a pen from his shirt pocket and wrote a few lines before handing it to her. "If you need anything…"

She looked at his home number and his and Ty's cell numbers, then nodded. "Thank you."

"We'll be checking by. Don't worry if you don't see us." For the first time, Maricci broke his professional demeanor with a grin that had probably stopped—or jump-started—a ton of female hearts. She wondered if the gold band on his left hand had slowed the fluttering any. "That's the point."

"Thanks," she said again. There was no overstating her gratitude that Decker had people he trusted, people she could trust.

The house was quiet once she locked up again. She walked into the living room to check out the juvenile messages on the walls, circled through the kitchen and came back to the end of the hall. After picking up the once-clean clothes and leaving them for another trip to the laundry room, she carried Decker's duffel upstairs, replacing the toiletries in the bathroom, going to his room to put away the clothes.

She stopped abruptly.

Instead of snoozing in bed, Decker was standing beside it. The clothing he'd worn that morning was on the floor, and now he wore olive drab shorts and held a short-sleeve shirt. The print was subdued for a Hawaiian shirt—exotic blue flowers and pale green leaves on an ivory background. It was so not his taste that she knew it must have been a gift.

From Cate. How could they have even vaguely considered marriage when she knew so little about him?

Masiela ignored the fact that his unfastened shorts rode low on his hips and went on into the room. She didn't notice that he had a great chest, smooth and muscled, or a nicely flat stomach. She didn't even give a hint of a thought to the knowledge that he had a great back, too, and that she'd always been a sucker for muscular backs. Nope, she paid none of that any mind.

She set the duffel on the dresser. "You should be in bed."

"I'm going to rest. Downstairs." He lifted the shirt. "A little help?"

Still doing a lot of ignoring, she closed the distance between them and took the shirt by the collar. "This is beyond help. I never thought I'd see the day when you'd wear something so…Hawaiian."

"It's the only clean shirt I stand a chance of getting on—" he extended his arm, and she guided the fabric carefully over the cast "—without hurting."

He shrugged his uninjured arm through, then pulled the edges together. She fastened the buttons, fixed her gaze on the center of a blue flower and slid her hands underneath the cool cotton to the waistband of his shorts. Her fingers grazed warm, bare skin, and her breath caught, or was it his?

The button slid easily through the hole, but she fumbled with the zipper. This time it was definitely *his* breath that caught, followed by an indistinguishable mutter that she suspected was a curse. Feeling his scowl, she glared at the flower in return. "Hey, I'm not used to zipping up in reverse."

Heat radiated from him as the zipper rasped to a stop. Immediately, he took a step away. If he hadn't moved, she would have. Since he had, she remained where she was, pretending a carelessness she didn't feel. "Tell me you didn't buy that shirt yourself."

He slid his feet into flip-flops. "In what universe would I pick this out?"

"Just because Dr. Cate can fix broken bones, it doesn't mean she can choose clothes."

"Don't I know it." He gestured toward her. "I need the sling."

The white cotton sling was on the bed behind her. She picked it up, helped him put it on, then positioned the foam cushion on his neck. She was about to make some inane remark when her gaze caught his. His hazel eyes were dark, shadowed, and his voice came out husky.

"Thanks."

She had trouble catching her breath. "You're welcome." She had more trouble tearing her gaze from his. Finally she remembered what she'd come in for—to put away the clothes he'd packed—and opened the duffel. Trying to sound at least somewhat normal, she said, "You know, if you called Cate to help you out, she would probably come."

Though her back was to him now, she could feel his stare. "We ended things last night, but I should call her asking favors? You used to give better advice than that, Mas."

We ended things last night. Had she needed to hear that there were no doubts, no maybes, no working it out? Not that it made a lot of difference. It didn't give

her the right to make a move of her own. It didn't mean
he wanted her to make a move. That tension just now
probably would have sparked between any man and
woman in the same situation. It didn't mean anything,
except that her libido was alive and well.

Seeking a distraction, she said, "I didn't give advice,
good or bad."

He snorted. "Right. 'Her IQ is smaller than her
bra size.' 'Do you have something against intelligent
conversation?' 'Pretty and smart are not mutually
exclusive, you know.'"

She left the empty duffel on the closet floor, then
faced him again. "Those were just statements of fact and
honest questions. You can't deny, your taste in women
was atrocious."

"I worked with pretty and smart eight to ten hours a
day, and I balanced it off the job with pretty and dumb.
What's wrong with that?"

He'd never called her pretty or smart that Masiela
could recall. Maybe "smart-ass" on occasion. But he'd
never given any hint that he thought she was at all
attractive, at least until the night he jumped her bones—
then pretended it didn't happen.

*Since you didn't say anything, I figured it would be
best to ignore it.*

She never would have guessed in a million years that
he'd wanted her to bring it up first. What would have
happened if she had? Would he have wanted to have sex
with her again? Was it possible he might even have asked
her out on a date? Been interested in a relationship?

Or said, "Hey, it was fun, but we can't do it again"?
Or, "It was a mistake. It won't happen again"?

Even though he'd said just this morning that he didn't
regret it.

That knowledge sent a warm little shiver through her. All these years she'd wondered and, considering how things had ended between them, had figured the answer was a resounding yes. Now she knew it wasn't. Despite the fact that he'd ended up angry and distrusting her, he didn't regret those few hours. That was incredible.

Chapter 9

Feeling unsettled, AJ brushed his teeth, splashed water on his face, then went downstairs, his left hand trailing the wall just in case. Masiela had already folded away the sofa bed and was in the kitchen, changed into shorts and a T-shirt that drew his gaze over long expanses of bronzed skin. There was a scar on her right knee, a souvenir from learning to ride a bike, and another on her left calf, the result of her first down-and-dirty fight on the job. She'd been about to handcuff a suspect when his buddy had come out of nowhere, knocked her to the ground and tried to grab her weapon. After breaking the guy's wrist with a wrist lock—AJ felt a twinge of sympathy—she used the weapon to hold them both until backup arrived, then she'd quietly driven herself to the hospital to get eight stitches in her leg.

She'd been the uncomplaining, I'll-take-care-of-myself type from the beginning.

Had she thought she could take care of the Brat Pack?

Assuming everything she'd told him about their harassment was true, she should have known the best way to deal with them: get herself wired. A case like that always came down to he said-she said, unless she was smart enough to get them on tape. Mas was definitely smart…though she hadn't come to him for help.

That still bothered him.

She had hot dogs sizzling in a skillet, buns toasting in another and was chopping onions and pickles to go with the sauerkraut heating on the back burner. Back in Dallas, he'd turned her on to coleslaw on her dogs, and she'd done the same for him with kraut and pickles.

Once everything was cooking or chopped, she stretched—nothing big or overdone, just hands curled into fists near her neck, elbows raised, back arched, all her muscles tightened, then relaxed. It was a purely utilitarian move that left him purely appreciative.

It was a sad thing when watching a woman stretch could make at least one part of his anatomy want to do the same.

"How's your arm?" she asked when she straightened. "Is it hurting?"

"Yeah." He didn't like whining, but it had been less than twenty-four hours, and he was damned tired of it all. Of having to either hurt badly or take medication that made him sleepy and/or loopy, of not even being able to open the bottle or get the drink of water that allowed him to take the damn medication.

"It probably wouldn't hurt if you took a couple more pills after lunch."

He winced at her use of the word *hurt,* and she rephrased. "It probably wouldn't matter if you took a couple more."

"Yeah, I will."

She fixed two glasses of iced tea, then dished up the hot dogs, automatically cutting his into manageable pieces. The first bite made his stomach flip-flop, the second settled it a bit and by the third he was already feeling better. He'd polished off the first and was starting the second when his mouth opened and, completely on its own, a question came out. "Why criminal defense?"

It wasn't the first time he'd asked. Hell, they'd had the discussion so many times he knew how it would go. He asked; she answered; he didn't get it. But maybe this time would be different. Maybe, knowing what he knew now, this time he would be willing to understand it.

Mas was quiet for a long time, her gaze fixed on the countertop between them. Finally she sighed, her shoulders shaking with the force of the exhalation. "I didn't have many problems when I started with the DPD. Oh, there was always the occasional officer who still believed women should be answering phones and making coffee, the one who didn't trust women to back him up, the one who especially didn't trust a Latina woman. For the most part, though, I was treated like anyone else."

AJ had never had a problem with female cops, but he'd worked with people who did. Even now, there were more than a few on the Copper Lake PD and the city council who'd disagreed with his decision to promote Kiki Isaacs to detective, not because they doubted her ability but because of her gender. They were the same ones who'd voiced disapproval over Ty Gadney's promotion because of his race. Some prejudices were hard to defeat.

"On the street, it was a different story. There were plenty of victims who didn't want to talk to the woman. They wanted a real cop. You know, a police*man*. There were suspects whose macho pride couldn't take being handcuffed and hauled off by a girl. Those people didn't bother me, though. Given enough time, women would win over the victims, and I could always kick the macho perp's ass."

She said it matter-of-factly, and he knew it was true. Even with the bastard twice her size who had blackened her eye, she'd still looked better than him when it was over.

"What did bother me were the little things. The patrol officer who used a pretext stop to meet a pretty girl or to harass someone who'd pissed off a buddy. The ones who got bored, so they picked some poor sucker to give a hard time. The ones who looked the other way when they stopped a DUI who happened to be a friend or relative or, worse, someone politically connected. The ones who got to a domestic dispute and took the husband or boyfriend aside to tell him that, yeah, she deserved a good smack, just do it someplace where it wasn't so obvious next time. The ones who were tired or frustrated or burned out or just didn't give a damn, who blew off the victims."

AJ wished for those extra pain pills now, to make him so goofy he didn't have to admit that her complaints were valid. He'd never done any of the things she mentioned— except for a pretext stop to meet a gorgeous blonde, way back in his first year on the department. But he'd known plenty of cops guilty of the others. Sometimes their action, or inaction, turned out to be harmless. Sometimes it hadn't. But it had always been wrong.

"Call me naïve," Mas went on, "but I believe cops should be held to a higher standard. They shouldn't get away with speeding or driving drunk or incompetence, just because they're on the job. They shouldn't pocket a little money during a drug bust or demand personal favors from informants or violate a suspect's civil rights during an interrogation. They shouldn't get away with perverting and breaking the law because they wear a badge."

"I agree," he said quietly. "A lot of cops take advantage of their authority. Some use it for their own gain, and a few flat-out abuse it. But you have to admit, overall, most cops are good, law-abiding officers."

She nodded, her black hair reflecting the lights overhead. "Mostly. But not when they ignore the activities of the ones who aren't. You know there were whispers about Myers, Kinney and Taylor, rumors about how they did their jobs, how they got their confessions. I heard them before I even got transferred into homicide. But everyone ignored them—*you* ignored them—because they were your buddies and they were getting results."

AJ gestured impatiently with his left hand. "There are always rumors. You think there weren't plenty about you and me? About why I took you on as partner? About what we did when we were off-duty?"

She tilted her head to one side. "I managed to miss out on those. Probably because, if the Brat Pack taught me anything, it was not to hang out with the guys unless *you* were there, too."

He'd never noticed back then, but hindsight was clearer. There'd always been open invitations within the squad—drinks at a bar down the street after work, cookouts, parties, going to games together. Masiela had never accepted or refused until he did, and he'd never arrived anywhere to find her already there. She always came after him and left with or before him.

Because she hadn't felt safe with their fellow cops.

She was smart—more than competent—she'd worn

the same badge they did, carried the same gun, had the same authority. She'd busted her ass to be in better shape than any of them, and she'd never backed down from an enraged drunk, doper, drug dealer or murderer. He'd always known that if she had his back, he was good.

But she hadn't felt safe with the detectives they worked with.

He hadn't had her back, and he'd never had a damn clue. How stupid could he have been?

"Everyone was big on results. The means justified the ends. Kinney, Myers and Taylor had a ninety-five-percent solve rate, so no one cared if they bent the rules now and then. If a suspect came out of interrogation with injuries he hadn't had going in. If witness accounts changed from seeing 'somebody' to a picture-perfect description of their prime suspect, if evidence that might be exculpatory got lost before reaching the defense attorney, they were taking bad guys off the street, and that was all anyone cared about."

She picked up the last bite of her hot dog, stared at it, then tossed it down again. Pushing the plate out of the way, she rested her arms on the countertop and leaned toward him. "I worked with some good cops, Decker, but I also worked with some damn bad ones. I saw how easy it was to railroad someone, to plant or destroy evidence. I saw people go to prison for long sentences who swore they were innocent, and I believed some of them, because I knew how people like Kinney manipulated the system. I knew he and his pals were more dangerous than most of the people they arrested.

"That's why I became a defense attorney."

In the silence that echoed, he admitted he'd been right: he got it this time. He was *willing* to get it. That didn't say much for the detective—or the man—he'd been back then.

"I'm sorry."

"I wish you'd had faith in me, Decker," she murmured.

AJ stared down at her. "I had faith in you, Mas. I trusted you with my life."

The smile that ghosted across her face was filled with regret and bitterness. "You trusted every officer on the Dallas Police Department with your life. But you didn't trust me enough to even consider what I was trying to tell you about the Rodriguez case. Even now, you don't trust me enough to look at the evidence I've gathered against your friends."

You made a rookie mistake, Decker, she'd said earlier. *You didn't look at the evidence. You didn't care if it was all just a little too neat.* He'd never given credence to her accusations before. The case had been put together by three experienced, highly regarded detectives; it had been bought off on by an experienced, highly regarded assistant DA, and the jury had needed only ninety minutes to find Israel Rodriguez guilty.

So it had been neat. She'd worked enough homicide cases to know that some of them were. Sometimes the obvious answer was the right one. Sometimes you were lucky enough to get witnesses, fingerprints, DNA and enough trace evidence to qualify as overkill.

Mas had been unable to accept that Teri's case had been one of those lucky ones.

And AJ had been unwilling to acknowledge that a career criminal like Israel Rodriguez didn't commit easy-to-solve crimes.

He ran his fingers across his hair, breathed heavily and opened his mouth to say, hell, he didn't know what, but she was already turning away from him toward the sink, clearly not expecting any sort of real answer.

She said they'd harassed her, but AJ had never noticed it.

She'd been wary of them, and he'd never noticed that, either.

Kinney had threatened her. Donovan had taken the threat seriously enough to move her out of state.

Why would they threaten her if there wasn't something to her evidence?

Most cops are good, he'd told her, and she'd solemnly added, *Not when they ignore the activities of the ones who aren't.*

She was right, of course, and he was guilty—of ignoring the rumors about the Brat Pack, of brushing off her initial dislike of them, of not trusting her. God knew, she'd earned it.

He was one of those bad cops who'd looked the other way.

But not anymore.

Wishing she could pull back the curtain over the kitchen sink and let a little light in, Masiela rinsed the lunch dishes, stacked them in the dishwasher, then took two tablets from the bottle of pain pills. When AJ came closer, she offered them.

He looked as if he wanted to argue that it wasn't time, that he was tough and strong and didn't need them. She cut him off with a blunt observation. "You look like hell, and I feel like it. We're tired. We need rest."

"I want to talk."

"Not now." She never thought he would ever be willing to hear her out and certainly never dreamed she would put him off if he was. But he did look worn out.

Pain etched his face, his skin had paled a few shades, and there was a fine tremor in his hand. And she did feel crappy. An adrenaline surge deserved a good rest afterward, and she hadn't gotten it. Whatever she'd been running on for the past few hours was sapped. All she wanted was to curl up, close her eyes and go brain-dead for a while.

AJ's expression was belligerent, but in the end, he washed down the pills with a gulp of tea, then rubbed his forehead. "Can you help me out of this shirt?"

Can't you just sleep in it? she wanted to ask. Helping him put it on had been intimate enough. Taking it off...

After a gulp of her own tea, she tried to close off that line of thought and lighten the mood. "Can I burn it afterward?"

"You can do whatever you want with it."

He was moving slowly as she followed him down the hall, up the stairs and into the bedroom. She straightened the covers, then positioned the pillows before moving back to his side of the bed.

Her fingers felt as stiff as his must after so long without use. They fumbled with the top button on the gaudy shirt, took their sweet time with the second and made her swear silently at the third. It was because she was tired, she told herself. Because she hadn't slept any better than he had last night. Because the incident of adolescent angst had, for a time, brought the fear back to heart-pumping life.

But the truth didn't want to be closed off. It was because she really wanted to touch him. To make this far more intimate than merely undressing him. To kiss that warm, bare skin. To rest her cheek against his shoulder and breathe in that old familiar scent. To remember when he'd touched her and held her and kissed her as if he just might die without her. To find out if he might touch her, hold her and kiss her like that again.

He swayed unsteadily, and his forehead bumped against hers. "Sorry," he mumbled. "I'm starting to see double, and that makes me a little unsteady."

"I know." Silently chastising herself, she made short work of the remaining buttons, removed the shirt, then efficiently, unemotionally, did the same with his shorts. Holding on to his good arm, she helped him into bed, fluffed the pillows beneath his cast and pulled the covers over him.

She was about to straighten and leave the room when his fingers caught her shirt, then slid up into her hair, around to her neck and pulled her closer. She braced herself with one hand. The last thing she needed was to tumble onto his arm.

Before she could ask what he was doing, his mouth touched hers, neither quick nor slow, hard nor soft, just a solid pressure, lips against lips, a platonic kiss. Then his tongue levered between her lips, dipping into her mouth, and her knees damn near gave way. There was no hurry, no desperation or need, just wanting. He wasn't going to die without her, or starve, or burst into flames.

No, the dying, starving, flame-bursting was all hers.

When he released her, his eyes remained closed. "Damn," was all he said, a hint of all his years in Texas creeping into the word, making it twice as long.

Yeah, *damn*.

"Get some sleep," she whispered, in a voice too thick and heavy to be her own.

She made it halfway down the stairs before stopping to sit, arms around her knees, on a bare-wood riser. Her lips still tingled. She was sure if she touched them, she would feel tiny little shocks in her fingertips.

It was an amazing thing—a kiss that could leave a thirty-six-year-old woman, with her share of sexual experience, barely able to stand. She felt tingly all over and hot and tender and needy.

Just the image she wanted of herself: needy for the man who'd come closest to breaking her heart. But she'd been needy before and would likely find herself back there again. She would survive.

She always did.

AJ slept pretty well, considering most of his nap had been occupied with erotic dreams. He never should have kissed Masiela just before falling asleep. Hell, he never should have kissed her at all. It had been a long time, and so much had changed between them. But not his wanting her, and apparently not her wanting him back.

And kissing her was still pretty damn good. He'd do it again in a heartbeat.

He managed to dress himself in running shorts and an old sleeveless T-shirt that was stretched out a size too big and so faded its color was indistinguishable. With proper shoes and socks, he'd be ready for a run, though just the thought of pounding the pavement made his wrist throb.

He put on flip-flops, then went to use the bathroom. He needed a shave but wasn't ready to put a left-handed razor to his throat. His hair was getting long, too, considering that for him, half an inch was long. He could use a shower, but he hadn't figured out yet how that was going to work, unless he dripped dry.

Or threw himself on Masiela's mercy. And he had a

pretty good idea where *that* would lead—an option that was sounding better every hour.

When he reached the bottom of the stairs, he stopped, just stood there listening, feeling, breathing. It was the same old house, but different. Something that smelled really good in the kitchen joined the usual scents of wood, dust and stripper. Instead of the silence he normally came home to, music played and a clear, slightly off-key alto sang along. There was another presence besides his own, one that felt...well, at home. That belonged.

Detouring into the living room, he looked once more at the painted messages there. "Srcew you." It brought a dry chuckle. Though Kinney, Myers and Taylor weren't the type to leave graffiti, if they ever did, they would probably misspell it, too. He'd spent a lot of years teaching them that "myself and my partner" was not a proper subject for any sentence, especially in an official report.

The kitchen and dining room were empty when he moved on, though he found the source of the good smells: a pot of chicken in golden broth bubbling on the stove.

The music came from the library, so he went there. Stepping into the doorway, he was treated to the sight of Masiela facing one wall of floor-to-ceiling shelves. High on her head, her hair was pulled into a ponytail that made her look about eighteen. Stained denim shorts and a T-shirt didn't add any years, and neither did the clunky sneakers that could be worn for anything but sneaking.

His gaze slid over her, from silky black hair to dark eyes, from high cheekbones and perfect nose to full, lush mouth. Just that look and he wanted to kiss her again, wanted to know if she'd let him, wanted to do it right this time.

But there were other, uglier things he had to do first.

"Are you meditating? Praying? Hoping the wood-stripper fairies visited while we were gone?"

She glanced at him. "Just seeing how much is left to do."

"You don't have to do it."

"It keeps me busy."

"I figure doing everything for me is keeping you busy enough."

"I don't have to do everything. You got dressed by yourself." She crouched in front of the can of stripper, unscrewing the top and wrinkling her nose delicately. "You've been going to the bathroom by yourself."

"Thank God for small blessings," he muttered.

She tugged on a pair of heavy-duty gloves, then began applying the stripper to a shelf. "It's actually kind of relaxing, especially now that I know it won't be Dr. Cate's office."

He looked at the shelves she'd finished, at all the hard work she'd done on a space she'd thought would belong to another woman. No way he would've put out all that effort on a room for some other guy in her life to use. "This thing with Cate—"

"Is none of my business."

"Yeah, right. You were sure as hell curious before it ended."

She acknowledged that with a shrug. "However, earlier this afternoon…"

Three simple little words to send heat spreading through his body and turn his voice rough. "You mean when I kissed you."

She glanced at him, her lips pursed to control a smile. "Actually, I meant when you were standing in the kitchen saying, 'I want to talk.'"

"Huh?" He'd had a buzz from the pain pills, but not so much that he couldn't tell she'd responded to the kiss. She hadn't pushed him away or said anything along the lines of *no, we shouldn't*. She'd liked it. She may have thought it was a bad idea, but she'd still liked it.

She was waiting for him to say something more. He leaned against the wall, repositioned his sling, then scratched behind his ear. It would have been an easier topic to pursue three hours ago, when the narcotics were pumping through his veins, when anything he said or didn't say could be blamed on them. Now he took a deep breath.

"You're right, Mas. It was too neat. I made a mistake. I want—" He broke off, feeling anger and guilt and reluctance and nausea and disloyalty, like a lousy friend and a lousier partner. The best way to deal with all that knotted in his stomach was to go ahead and do whatever the hell it was he dreaded, so he took a deep breath, then said flatly, "I want to know what you've got."

He half-expected some show of triumph or smugness from her. Instead, she looked serious and…he didn't know, maybe *touched*. "Thank you," she murmured.

She turned back to the shelf, testing a patch, then carefully scraping off the stripper and layers of gunk. Had she learned that meticulousness from her mother, who spent her days moving mountains of dirt and rock with a soft brush and a trowel, to find the fragile secrets buried beneath?

Silently he scoffed. He wasn't sure Carmen Leal had taught her daughter anything besides the lesson that she wasn't important in her mother's life.

And yet, good or bad, she'd always been important in *his* life.

The task done, she removed the gloves and left the room, passing close enough for him to feel the air stir. He followed her into the kitchen, where she unzipped the computer case, set the laptop on the counter and powered it up.

"Everything I have has been input or scanned into the computer," she said quietly. "I've got original documents stashed in a safe deposit box, and there are copies of this file at my office, on the Internet and in my post office box."

"And with Donovan."

She nodded.

"They'll expect copies."

"They'll also expect anyone who finds one to be too afraid to do anything with it."

Maybe that would have been true…before now. If they'd killed her, what were the odds Donovan would have pursued the case? Would he have risked his life against cops who killed to achieve their goals? Maybe, maybe not.

But AJ would. He would make it his life's goal to see them punished.

Her hand hovered over the keyboard. He knew her too well—knew she was second-guessing. Was it enough to her that he was willing to listen, that he was considering the possibility that his buddies were guilty? Was she thinking that the less he knew, the safer he might be?

He laid his hand over hers, stilling the tremors. "Don't back out, Mas. It took you eight years to get me to this point. Show me what you have."

She curved her fingers around his for a moment, then pulled free and opened the password-protected file.

Leaving it open on the screen, she went to the stove to check on dinner. "You know the theory: Teri was leaving town, and she told Rodriguez. He didn't like to let his women go, they argued and he threw her off that rooftop. Witnesses placed them together just before the murder, on a street corner and at a diner, and he was stopped a few blocks away shortly after."

AJ nodded. Myers had called him, and he'd gone to the scene, arriving in time to see the paramedics cover Teri's body. He'd watched the initial interview with Rodriguez and stayed updated on the following investigation.

"According to the reports, there were nine people in the diner, but Donovan called only one, the cook. I tried to interview the others, but the information the police had gathered on them was incomplete—the wrong addresses for four, none for another. No phone numbers for three of them. Two were common names that belonged to dozens of people in the Dallas area, and had no identifying information to narrow it down. The two waitresses both quit their jobs after the murder and left with no forwarding addresses. When I interviewed their families and friends, they wouldn't even admit that the women existed."

While she talked, she melted butter and stirred in cocoa, then added it to flour and other stuff. Now she stirred in walnuts and miniature marshmallows before buttering a foil pan, then scraping it all in. Brownies had always been one of AJ's favorite desserts, especially Masiela's brownies. He'd missed it when she stopped baking them for him.

He'd missed a hell of a lot because of his hardheadedness.

He refocused on the conversation. "You know the neighborhood where that diner was, the kind of customers they get—the kind that don't like to get involved with the cops. The waitresses both had records. The customers probably did, too."

"Probably. Which doesn't justify the officers' failure to properly ID them." After sliding the brownies into the oven, she removed chicken wings from the broth on the stove and dumped in a bag of frozen dumplings. "We both know people lie, that not everyone has a driver's license or carries ID. But failing to identify six out of nine witnesses?"

She stopped what she was doing, meeting his gaze squarely. "How often does that legitimately happen, Decker?"

Chapter 10

Decker didn't answer. Instead, he sat staring at the computer screen, but he wasn't reading the text there. He was still listening, though, and Masiela was grateful for that.

She gave the dumplings a stir, then faced him across the counter. "Did you ever go in the diner? It isn't one of those where the kitchen is open to the dining room. It's in back, with a pass-through window. You don't have much of a view of the tables through that window. And yet, with eight people who were actually supposedly in the room with Rodriguez and Teri, the only witness Donovan called was the one who wasn't.

"I finally found one of the waitresses working in Houston. She wouldn't contradict the cook's testimony, but she wouldn't confirm it, either. Two years after the trial, and she was still scared. She insisted she didn't know anything about that night, and when I went back to talk to her again, she was gone. Again."

"What about the people who saw them arguing on the street?" His voice was grim, not argumentative, not hostile, just flat and stiff, asking for answers he knew he wasn't going to like.

"Phyllis Jackson and Manny Guzman. They were standing on the corner, waiting for a friend to pick them up. They were good witnesses. They told exactly the same story every single time. At best, they rehearsed it. At worst, they were given a script to memorize."

It wouldn't have been hard for the detectives to find people willing to lie for them. Honesty wasn't a big deal to most of the people they dealt with. Some told little lies; others, with the right incentive—the right reward, the right threat—would tell really big ones.

"It took me a long time to find out that Jackson wasn't Phyllis's real name. It's Watson, and Troy Watson is her older brother. You remember him."

The corners of Decker's mouth pinched. "Hell, I only busted him four, five times."

Like Rodriguez, Watson ran prostitutes, but he also dealt drugs on the side. Besides the business competition, there'd been some personal hostility between them, too. With Rodriguez out of the way, Watson had expanded his business and, presumably, gotten payback for the personal issue, as well.

Finally Decker looked up at her. He was clearly trying hard to control his expression and keep it blank, but he couldn't tamp down the emotion in his eyes. Anger, regret, disappointment, disgust. "What else?"

"The police stopped Rodriguez a few blocks away from the murder scene. Routine traffic stop for a broken taillight."

Decker nodded. "He claimed he'd gotten a message from one of his girls to pick her up over there. She denied it."

"Yeah. A thousand-dollar deposit was made to her mother's bank account the week after she testified. Mom claimed she didn't know where it came from, and unfortunately, daughter died of an overdose a few days later." She began stripping the small chunks of meat from the chicken wings, dropping them into the stock pot. "As for the guy Rodriguez said delivered the message, I couldn't locate him. He'd disappeared immediately after the murder. Dopers go missing, you know. Either they turn up after a while or they don't. No big loss."

For a few minutes she worked in silence, and Decker let her. They both knew the best—or worst, depending on point of view—was coming, and neither was in a rush to get there. So far, everything she'd told him had merely pointed to a sloppy investigation. The next part pointed to his friends.

She stripped the last wing, then washed and dried her hands. Slowly, she circled the peninsula, sat down next to Decker and opened the media player on the computer, then clicked on a video file.

"Three months ago I found him. He's been living in California all these years. This is what he told me." She didn't click on the Play button, but waited, hands clasped, for Decker to do it. It took him a minute, but finally he did.

Brian Brown was only twenty-six years old, but they'd been a tough twenty-six years. He was a recreational drug user, back when he'd gotten caught up in Teri's murder, but since then it had become hard-core. He slept in shelters or on the streets, ate at soup kitchens, stole whatever else he needed and blew the occasional money sent by his more respectable sister on drugs, booze and parties. It was only the sister getting fed up with his choices that had enabled Masiela to find and interview him.

She sat through the interview, asking questions, and had watched it a dozen times since. She didn't watch now, but closed her eyes and listened to the voices—hers quiet and calm, his edgy. He was always edgy, except when he scored.

"They picked me up the night before and said—"

"Who picked you up?" she interrupted.

"Them three cops that was always hanging out together. One of 'em was named Myers, and another was Taylor. The other one, he always shaved his head and wore these mirrored sunglasses. Anyways, they picked me up and said they was takin' me in, and I told 'em, I ain't done nothin' wrong, and that one with the sunglasses, he said, 'Hell, son, you was born doin' somethin' wrong.' But he says maybe I can do 'em a favor this time, and I wouldn't have to go jail."

"What kind of favor?"

Brown squirmed in his chair. The interview had taken place in her L.A. hotel room, with a poorly done still life on the wall behind him. Even though the room was midprice and nothing special, he looked distinctly out of place.

"Wasn't nothin' much. They just wanted me to take a message to Izzy the next night—tell 'im that Shawna got stuck over on Rosetta and needed a ride. That was all."

"And in exchange for that, they wouldn't arrest you?"

His head bobbed.

"Anything else?"

"Officer Myers, he give me a bus ticket to Chicago. Said he knew I had family there. And Taylor, he give me five hundred dollars. To make a new start, he said. Far away from Dallas. The ticket weren't in my name. They give me a fake ID, too. Charles Carter."

"So you went to Chicago?"

"Hell, no. You think I wanna lie to Izzy, then have them cops know where I was? I sold the ticket and the ID and come out here. It's a lot harder to find someone in a place like L.A., and I did *not* want them cops or Izzy to find me."

Decker stopped the video, got to his feet and paced across the room, his footsteps heavy and slow. He pivoted into the kitchen, stared down at the bubbling chicken and dumplings, then bleakly faced her. "Why Teri? Why not one of the other girls?"

Everyone believed Rodriguez had killed another of his girls for trying to leave him, and Teri had been planning to do the same. Decker had known it, and he'd told Masiela. It was pretty good odds that he'd mentioned it in front of Myers and company. They all worked together; they were buds; they had no secrets.

At least, that Decker had been aware of.

"I think she was just convenient. In the wrong place at the wrong time."

"They just needed one of Rodriguez's girls, and she was there? She could make a pattern for them?" He dragged his hand over his hair. "Jesus, did I tell them she was quitting? Did I cause—"

"*No.* Decker, you weren't the only person Teri talked to. Others knew she wanted out. Hell, it's a fair bet that all of them want out at some point. But the only people who bear any blame are the ones who threw her off that roof. No one forced them to do it. They had their own reasons, and they chose their actions."

He looked so disillusioned that she wanted to circle the counter and wrap her arms around him. She stayed where she was, though, watching him, waiting. He was trying to turn off the emotion, to take a step back, forget his connections to the victim and the detectives and look at the case as nothing more than a case. To some degree, he succeeded.

"So…with only one witness out of nine telling the prosecution's story, the whole diner thing is questionable," he said quietly, thinking out loud more than talking to her. "Phyllis Jackson's relationship to Troy Watson makes her testimony less than reliable, and Manny Guzman's relationship with Phyllis discounts his. Brown's story supports Rodriguez's, but it's a doper's word against three cops. There's no proof."

"Other than the fact that a Charles Carter did take the bus from Dallas to Chicago on the date Brown says he was supposed to." She leaned back in the chair and folded her arms across her middle. "There's no smoking gun. I can't put those cops on the rooftop with Teri. I can't prove they killed her, but I think I can prove reasonable doubt that Rodriguez killed her. And, with the phone threat from Kinney and the other stuff, I think I can make a decent case that, for whatever reason, they don't want me to clear him."

The timer went off, beeping loudly while she and Decker held gazes. Finally, she went to take the brownies from the oven. Using a dish towel for a pot holder, she set the pan on the back burner to cool, then turned off the heat under the dumplings. "Dinner is ready. Think you can stomach it?"

AJ smiled weakly. "I can always eat." It was something

every homicide detective learned, to leave a gruesome murder scene, put the violence out of mind and grab a meal before going out again.

Despite his words, though, when they sat down, for the first few minutes they both just picked at their food.

Finally, AJ put his fork down and locked gazes with her. "What about motive? Why would they want to frame Rodriguez badly enough to kill Teri?"

"I don't know. Maybe it was because they could never nail him on that other murder. They took it personally that they couldn't make a case against him. They didn't give a damn about justice for the dead girl. They just wanted to beat Rodriguez. They wanted another check in the 'closed' column." She picked up her glass in both hands, appreciating the cool damp against her fingers. "Maybe they did it just because they could. Just to prove to themselves that they could commit a murder, frame someone else for it and walk away heroes for having solved it."

"Maybe Rodriguez is the one who happened to be convenient," AJ said. "Maybe their problem was with Teri. Maybe she knew something that made her a threat. They decided to get rid of her and saw a chance to get Rodriguez, too. Payback for that other case."

"There are any number of possibilities," Masiela agreed. "Probably the only people who know for sure are Myers, Kinney and Taylor, and they're not eager to share."

Decker picked up the fork again and ate for a time, spearing dumplings too fat and slippery for a spoon. He made an appreciative gesture—this guy with the cast-iron stomach who would eat pretty much anything anyone made for him—and a faint flush of pleasure warmed her. She knew she was a good cook, but she loved every bit of flattery.

After a moment, he stopped for a drink of pop. "The trial ended six years ago. Why did you keep looking into it? Why didn't you let it go?"

"Because I believed my client was innocent." She took a bite and chewed it thoroughly before finally, ruefully adding, "Because I had serious problems with the detectives. You were right. I didn't like them, I didn't trust them and I wanted to prove that they'd lied."

It was the first time she'd ever said it out loud. Granted, the weaknesses of the case had caught her attention, and she'd done her best to find answers before the trial. But she had to admit, it wasn't merely justice for Rodriguez that had kept her going; it was also the fact that getting justice for him meant exposing the detectives for the arrogant, corrupt bastards they were.

"I'd be ashamed of my pettiness if I hadn't proven I was right."

"You always had good instincts."

"I trained with the best."

He shook his head. "But I missed all this."

"It wasn't your case. You were grieving. You had reason to believe that your fellow detectives were doing their job the way you'd do it."

"You tried to tell me…."

"You had a lot of years on the department with those guys. I had nothing but a feeling." Decker had always counseled her to trust her gut. Even if everything pointed *this* way, if her gut was leading her *that* way, that was the way she needed to go. "Besides," she said, forcing a lighter tone into her voice, "you were already angry with me for turning down that job offer from the DA's office and for taking the case in the first place."

The glare he turned on her had stopped stronger people in their tracks. "I was a cop. Evidence is all that matters to a good cop, not someone's spin on it. I let Kinney and Taylor and Myers tell me what they wanted me to know. I didn't look closer, even when you tried to get me to. I should have. Damn it, I should have."

Masiela pushed her bowl away and rested her arms on the counter, leaning toward him. "You can blame yourself all day, Decker, and all it does is make you feel bad. There was a time when I would have settled for you being in a permanent funk, but it's long past. Look at the evidence now. Read the interviews. Finish the video. Tell me what I've overlooked, where I need to go next."

He didn't hesitate. "Leave it in Donovan's hands. He's a smart guy. He'll recognize the problems, and he'll do the right thing."

"I'm smart, too."

"Yeah, but it's liable to get you killed. They won't go after the DA's office. You're a much easier target."

He was thinking the worst of his old buddies, and worrying about her. The knowledge went a long way in easing the tension that had knotted through her during the conversation. She'd waited so long for that kind of validation—and that, she realized, was another thing that had kept her investigating long after her client went to prison. She'd wanted to expose the bastards not just to the world at large, but to Decker. She'd wanted to prove to him that she'd made the right choice, that there were innocent people charged with crimes by ineffective or dirty cops, and that they needed her, an ex-cop who knew how the system worked, to get justice.

She'd wanted Decker's approval.

After supper, AJ settled on the couch, the computer on his lap, scrolling through Masiela's file. He didn't read everything. There were hundreds of pages, along with video and audio recordings and copies of official reports. He started to page past a newspaper article, caught the date in the corner of his eye and stopped. It was from the *Dallas Morning News* and showed a photograph of Rodriguez's first—only?—homicide victim. The murder had taken place fourteen months before Teri died, and the reporter had done a follow-up before-she's-forgotten piece. He'd interviewed the victim's family, the police, Rodriguez, his lawyer and Donovan, and he ended the story with a quote from Dave Kinney: "We're gonna get him. We promise."

On its own, it didn't look bad. Reassurance to the family that they'd be keeping their eyes on the bastard who killed their daughter and dumped her body in a salvage yard like she was just so much trash. AJ had said the words to other families himself; it was the kind of reassurance they needed, even if there was little chance of making good on it.

Knowing what he knew now, it seemed more ominous.

Continuing through the pages, he found photographs of the three detectives outside the courthouse following Rodriguez's guilty verdict. They were victorious, hugging each other, grinning ear to ear, celebrating with the small group of cops around them. Only Myers seemed different. Oh, he was grinning, one fist pumped into the air, but his gaze was directed off to the side, out of the shot, and he looked smug. Threatening.

The dishwasher rumbled to life, then Masiela came around to sit on the couch beside him, close enough to see the screen. Her nose wrinkled slightly.

"You remember that moment?"

"I do. I was standing right here." She gestured in the

air to screen left—exactly where Myers was looking. "I felt my skin crawling, and I glanced up and locked gazes with him."

"Were you scared?"

Even now a slight shiver ran through her. "Yeah."

"But not enough to come to me."

"I was here—" she patted the air again "—and you were there." One rounded nail touched the top right corner of the screen. "It doesn't look like a lot of distance, but it felt like about six million miles."

He hadn't noticed himself in the shot. He was apart from all the cops, standing halfway up the courthouse steps with Teri's cousin from Kansas, the only relative willing to take Teri's daughter. She'd come for the trial, but she hadn't brought little Morgan with her. She just wanted to be satisfied, she'd said, that the man who'd killed Teri had gotten what he deserved.

And AJ had assured her that he had.

"I hate being so damn stupid."

Masiela, close enough that her sleeve brushed his arm when she shrugged, was philosophical. "Sometimes you know all the answers. Sometimes you can't see what's in front of your nose."

And what was in front of his nose right now was Mas—beautiful, soft, sexy, passionate, warm. The only bright light in all this crap. In all those years, he'd never gotten over losing her, had never forgotten how much he loved her, depended on her. Not in a romantic sense, though there'd been that, too. After that one night together, after she'd pretended nothing had happened, he tried not to think of her that way, but the memory had always been there. The desire.

More desire with every passing moment.

He closed the laptop and carefully set it on the floor. "I can't think about that anymore."

"It wears you down after a while," Masiela agreed. "You have to get all that ugliness out of your head from time to time."

"How do you do it?"

"I visit Yelina and her girls, or drop in on Elian and his *chica* of the month. I sneak my grandmothers out of the retirement home for a day of shopping and seeing who can flirt with the most men."

He chuckled at the thought of her competitive grandmothers putting the moves on the men unlucky enough to cross their path. "You used to run my ass off when you needed a break."

"Yeah. That was before you started running *from* me instead of *with* me." She said it carelessly, but there was a flash of hurt in her eyes, gone quickly, but there long enough to make him hot with shame.

He twisted on the couch so he faced her and touched his left hand gently to her cheek. "I really am sorry."

"So am I. I was so used to you taking me seriously. I thought our friendship was too strong to be threatened by my switching jobs."

His brows raised. "You didn't just switch jobs, Mas. You went from hunting down murderers to trying to get them off. And you did it all on your own. You didn't discuss it with me. One day I'm thinking you're doing your final interview with the DA's office, and you come to dinner that night, saying, 'Hey, I took a job with a criminal defense firm'."

He'd been surprised as hell, but hurt, too. Prosecution and defense weren't just different sides of the same legal coin; to a homicide cop like him, they were different universes. Going to work for the opposing team was like giving up everything you believed in for better pay. It had been a huge decision—a wrong one, he'd been sure at the time—and one she'd made without even talking to him.

"It wasn't an easy choice, and I knew you wouldn't approve."

"Maybe if you'd discussed it with me, I could have at least tried to understand."

"And if I'd told you that the first big case I was looking at was Rodriguez's…would you have tried to understand that, too?"

Grimly, he shook his head. "You knew what it meant to me. You knew how I felt about Teri."

"Yeah. And how you felt about that—about her—trumped how you felt about me."

It wasn't that simple. Nothing about the whole mess was. Not even how he felt about Masiela right now. He wanted to have great handicapped sex with her. If he could keep her around long enough, he'd like to have great unhandicapped sex with her. He wanted to keep her safe, wanted Myers, Kinney and Taylor to pay for what they'd done not only to Teri and Rodriguez, but also to Mas. He wanted her back in his life, wanted to be able to turn to her whenever he needed to talk, wanted to know she had his back again, while he had hers.

Jeez, what he really wanted right this minute was to kiss her.

"How I felt about you," he repeated, his voice hoarse. "I felt like I'd lost my other half. You were damn near everything to me, Mas. My partner, my best friend, my once and future one-night stand, because you know, if it happened once, it was gonna happen again. When I wanted advice or help, someone to talk to, someone to listen to, someone to make me feel better or put things into perspective, someone who understood what I needed without me having to say a word—that was you. I didn't have anyone else remotely like you to go to."

He hesitated, considering those last words. "I've never had anyone else like you."

And that was as good a time to kiss her as any. He grasped her shoulder and pulled her toward him, leaning forward to meet her. She came willingly, raising her hands to his face, cupping his cheek with one hand, sliding the other around to his neck. She made a soft whimper the instant his mouth touched hers, but it wasn't a *don't do this* sort of plea. He knew, because he made the same sound.

He slid his tongue inside her mouth, bringing back flashes of that first time. She'd had too much to drink, and he'd stayed sober to drive her home. He'd walked her to her condo, unlocked the door for her and gone inside, thinking he'd make sure she was settled before leaving again. She'd thanked him for the ride with a hiccup, and then…

Even then he hadn't known how it happened. One moment they'd been looking at each other, and the next they'd been kissing as if their lives depended on it. It had changed everything.

Just as this would change everything.

It was awkward, having only one hand to touch her with. His fingers wrapped in her hair, slid along her spine, urged her nearer until she was straddling his legs, her breasts brushing his chest. His erection swelled, hard and achy, tormented by the slight movements of her hips rubbing against it.

His mind went dull, made hazy by feeling. Dimly, he was aware of his T-shirt being pulled over his head, of helping Mas do the same with hers. He fumbled left-handed with the button of her shorts, then concentrated instead on unfastening her bra while she shimmied out of her shorts.

For a moment he forced a stop so he could look at her. Her hair had come out of its ponytail and hung in a tangle around her shoulders. Her eyes were dark with passion, her lips slightly parted. He touched one fingertip to her mouth, and she closed her teeth on it, a sharp ache followed by the slow stroke of her tongue. It made his breath catch and left his voice hoarse. "You are so damn beautiful."

Her cheeks flushed a deeper bronze. "I bet you say that to all the girls who sit naked on top of you."

"You're not naked," he pointed out, and she wiggled around, bringing a groan from him, before dropping her panties to the floor.

He let his gaze slide slowly down, past the hollow at the base of her throat where her pulse was beating rapidly. Over her collarbones to the smooth, dark skin that swelled into her breasts, her nipples rosy-brown and standing erect. Across her flat middle and narrow waist, the curve of her hips, to the nest of curls and long, lean thighs.

He groaned again. "We should go upstairs." The couch was barely wide enough and lacked the comfort of his bed.

"I'll race you," she replied, but the only move she made was to rise onto her knees and hook her fingers in the waistbands of his shorts and briefs. She peeled them both off, adding them to the pile of clothes on the floor, then leaned forward, nuzzling his throat, leaving kisses along his jaw before taking his mouth in another hungry kiss.

His erection strained for her. Hand on her hip, he

guided her back down, then arched up to fill her. She was tight, hot, and he remembered clearly what he'd thought the first time.

Mine.

The idea sent a shudder through him and left him too damn close to coming too damn quick. He fought it, his muscles taut, his breathing labored, and thought he'd succeeded in at least a temporary delay when she broke the kiss, moved her mouth to his ear and whispered, "Come inside me, AJ. Please."

How could he refuse a request like that? He did come, and she did, too, great shivers racking her body, turning her breathing to ragged gasps, raising a flush of perspiration on her skin. She sagged against him, her forehead on his shoulder, her breath soft puffs against his skin.

Outside, thunder sounded not too far to the northwest. The air out there was probably electric with the promise of the oncoming storm. Inside, it was warm and steamy and so damn… He couldn't think of any other word but *right.* Sappy, but true.

He shifted onto his side, sliding his left arm under her, making room for her between his body and the cushions. "You called me AJ."

Her lashes fluttered open, and her dark eyes fixed on him, still hazy, but with the addition of satisfaction now. "I've called you that before."

"Yeah. The first day we met. The first time we had sex. The first night here, when you almost shot me."

"Yeah, well, calling you by your last name when we're naked and sweaty and you're inside me seems a little too impersonal." She paused. "Do you prefer impersonal?"

He moved his hips against hers. He may have come

once, but he wasn't finished. "I like being damn personal. I'd also like to go upstairs now."

Her smile was smug. "Am I invited, too?"

"Don't play dense, Mas. I may have a broken wrist, but I can still do a fireman's carry with my left arm."

She scoffed. "Like you've ever had to carry a woman to get her into your bedroom. Back in Dallas, they were lining up for the chance."

"You had your share of men. I think I went to dinner with every one of them at least once, especially on the first dates."

"Yeah, and you didn't like any of them."

"I liked some of them just fine. Just not with you." He had always told her none of them were good enough for her, part joke, part brotherly concern. Now he wondered if it had been possessiveness masquerading as joke and concern. Even then, before their night together, had he subconsciously wanted to remain the most important guy in her life?

"I don't do that anymore," he said. "The women."

She trailed her long fingers up his arm, then gave his shoulder a few deep squeezes. "A guy can only take so much indiscriminate sex, huh?"

He tilted his head, giving her access to the tight muscles in his neck. "Something like that. Don't laugh at this, but I found out I needed something more. Not just good sex and fun times, but someone to be everything you—"

He broke off so suddenly that the silence echoed in his ears. *Someone to be everything you were.* Best friend, confidant, most important person in his life. He'd had the perfect relationship with Mas, except for the lack of sex, and he'd gotten that from the regularly changing girlfriends. But once Mas was gone, he hadn't needed just casual sex; he'd needed someone to replace *her.*

No wonder he'd failed.

She swallowed hard, and he'd swear in the shadowy light that there were tears in her eyes. "Jeez, Decker," she mumbled, then pressed a kiss to his jaw. "That's the nicest thing you've never quite said to me."

Thunder continued to rumble as they made their way upstairs. Masiela carried their clothes and led the way, AJ a few steps behind.

"You always did like to lead," he commented. "Into buildings, crime scenes, dangerous situations. Back then I used to worry. Today, it's nice to be following."

She put a little extra sway into her hips as she climbed the last step. "You shouldn't have worried. I was very careful."

"Yeah, but even careful cops can get killed."

She shrugged. It was true, but back then she'd had a mix of adrenaline-fueled ballsiness combined with utter confidence in herself and her partner. She hadn't been scared. "There were a few times I would have happily given Dave Kinney or Stan Myers the lead, but did you ever notice that they always lagged behind?"

"Maybe they liked watching you move, too." Then his voice hardened. "Or they were just gutless bastards who didn't want to be first in with a suspect who was armed and likely to fire the first shot."

She felt matching twinges—gratitude that he believed her now, regret that he'd had to be disillusioned to get to that point. She was saved a response, though, by reaching the bedroom. As thunder boomed again, she opened the blinds to reveal whipping tree branches and an angry sky, thin patches of blue quickly giving way to puffy black clouds.

She pulled back the covers on the unmade bed, dumping them into a pile on the chair, then moved around to take AJ's hand, drawing him toward the bed.

Tugging back, he detoured to the night table, where a box of condoms occupied the front corner of the top drawer. She looked at them, mouth pursed. "Don't you think it's a little late?"

"It's never too late to decrease the odds. One time without is risky. Twice without is twice as risky. And five times..."

A grin spread across her face. "Feeling awfully confident for a guy with a recently broken wrist, aren't you?"

He dropped a handful of condoms on the nightstand. "Just thinking how many times will be enough."

She swallowed, and her stomach clenched. Suddenly she felt very naked. "And you're thinking five?"

Looking absolutely clueless regarding the knot in her stomach, he grinned. "For tonight."

Warmth seeped through her. She would like promises for much longer, but in the end, *tonight* was all she could ask for.

She touched his cheek, rubbing across his bristled jaw. "Decker—"

"AJ."

"AJ," she repeated. Her throat was choked, her lungs tight. She gazed down his body—incredibly nice chest, flat stomach, impressive erection, muscular legs—and forgot about talking. Drawing him close, she murmured against his mouth, "Four to go, partner. We'd better get started."

He advanced on her, and she backed up until the bed

bumped the back of her knees. She climbed onto the mattress, and he came after her, his muscles rippling, his look intense. That first night, the only light had been a nightlight in the corner farthest from her bed, enough to see by, not enough to see *too* much. Any moment she'd expected levelheaded bud Decker to snap to, explain why they couldn't go any further than the kisses they'd already shared, then beat it the hell out of there.

Tonight it was nice to have the overhead lights and time and the assurance that, no matter what might happen later, AJ wasn't going anywhere. His home this time. His bed. The most incredible look of hunger on his face.

When he cornered her, she lay on her back, but logistics failed them. If he rested on his left side, it left only his casted arm to touch her, and lying on his right side put too much pressure on his sore wrist. With a laugh, she gently pushed his shoulder, forcing him onto his back. "Ooh, I get to be on top again. What a hardship for me."

Kneeling between his legs, she leaned far forward and kissed his mouth, his jaw, the base of his throat. She gave a moment's attention to his left nipple, then to the right, then left a long trail of wet kisses across his stomach, his abs, the muscle that ridged his thigh.

Plastic crinkled, then appeared before her eyes. "Before it's too late," AJ said, his voice harsh.

She eyed the condom, then tore open the package and held it in two fingers. To her way of thinking, if she put it on, it was already too late. She was thirty-six and wanted to have babies, and she couldn't imagine a better father for at least the first one than AJ Decker. Even if things didn't work out between them, if she stayed in Dallas and he stayed in Copper Lake and these days were nothing more than a moment out of time, having a child would be an incredible gift.

And getting pregnant with his child without his agreement would be so wrong.

She unrolled the condom into place with as much touching, stroking and kissing as possible, leaving him hot and hard, and she climbed astride and slid herself into place, making herself hot and melty-soft. When he touched his hand to her thigh, she damn near sizzled, her nerves firing millions of tiny little explosions, and when he sucked her nipple into his mouth, she whimpered at the intensity of it.

Four to go. Dear God, she hoped she survived it.

Chapter 11

Friday afternoon was dark, rainy and even steamier than usual. Though the storm had passed soon after they'd gone to bed, the rain hadn't yet stopped pounding the earth, providing a sound track to everything they'd done. Masiela hoped the yapper Pepper next door had gotten a good soaking—and was inside now, dry and snoozing.

She and AJ had passed a leisurely morning making love, showering, dressing and eating lunch—and spent most of the afternoon on the couch, the computer between them, reading, discussing, arguing their way through her evidence. Now he set the computer on the coffee table and picked up the coffee she'd made an hour earlier.

"Give me that. I'll make fresh."

"Just stick it in the microwave for a minute."

Making a face at him, she took their cups into the kitchen and set them both in the sink. Within a minute, she had fresh coffee brewing and was filling a glass with iced tea for herself. "Leave the cast alone," she admonished without looking at him. He'd reached the cranky stage: if his wrist didn't hurt unbearably, if the cast didn't hamper everything he tried to do, then his arm itched down inside it enough to drive him crazy.

His gaze narrowed, and his clean-shaven jaw—he'd actually trusted her with his razor in the shower—set stubbornly. "It itches," he said for the tenth time.

"Yelina found an ivory chopstick worked wonders."

His scowl drew his brows tighter. "Yeah, sure, just let me pull one out of my chopstick drawer. You have any *reasonable* ideas?"

She carried a plate of leftover brownies to the couch, leaning past him to set them on the table. With a sweet smile, she said, "I can make you forget that it itches." Deliberately, she ran her tongue over her lips, leaving them shiny and moist—and his expression turned dry.

"Yeah, you could finish what you started in the shower," he said, his voice parched.

Her smile got sweeter. "Or I could smack you with a cast-iron skillet. That would make you forget a little itch." She swatted his leg. "Man up, Decker. Your little cousin Yelina didn't—"

He made an obscene gesture with his good hand, and she laughed. God, it felt good to laugh.

Once she was back with the coffee and tea and they'd each eaten a brownie or two, the mood grew somber again. "Donovan won't be happy that there's enough evidence to get a new trial for Rodriguez, but not enough to get the real killers," she remarked.

"But getting Rodriguez a new trial—and an acquittal—is your goal. Let DPD be responsible for anything more."

"If DPD hadn't been involved in the first place, Rodriguez would never have been charged. Unless Donovan can find something substantive to use against the Brat Pack, it's going to be business as usual in homicide."

"Maybe he'll find it. He's got access to stuff you don't."

She shifted on the sofa to face AJ. She'd worried the day before that convincing him the cops were involved in Teri's death would draw him in, that he wouldn't rest until they were punished. But right now, he was looking as if the case interested him only in a general cop sort of way, not as if he had any personal stake in it. "You could live with them getting away with Teri's murder?"

"If it keeps you safe, yeah."

The simple, flat answer touched her deeply. It didn't come from Decker her ex-partner but AJ, the man who'd broken her heart and done a pretty good job of mending it again.

But right now she needed Decker the ex-partner, not AJ the lover.

She made an effort to inject a careless, casual tone into her voice. "Then you wouldn't be too thrilled with the idea of setting me up as a target for them, would you?"

He slowly brought his gaze to hers. She'd seen the look plenty of times before, but it had never been directed at her. It was the *Jesus, you can't be that effin' stupid* look, the one reserved for the most moronic of criminals, cops and civilians alike.

"Remember why you're here? Phone call, break-in, gunshot? You're already a target." His voice was sharp with scorn, echoed in the thin curl of his mouth.

"I'm a target they can't find. If they *could* find me—"

"No."

"—then they'd be reckless enough to try something—"

"No."

"—and we'd be ready. *You'd* be ready. You'd catch them."

"I said no, damn it!"

His shout vibrated the very air, skittering along her bare arms, making her instinctively shrink back. They stared at each other, Mas surprised, AJ revealing such raw emotion. He wanted—needed—to protect her, she realized. Needed her to survive this unscathed. Unlike the last woman he'd tried to protect.

She reached for his hand. "AJ, I'm not Teri."

He continued to stare, but with cynicism in his hazel eyes. "You think I'm confusing you with my hooker-doper-informant?"

God, she hoped not. "You felt responsible for her. You made keeping her safe your job, and she died anyway. But I'm not like her. I'm not your responsibility."

He straightened his shoulders. "No, Mas, you're my life, and damned if I'm going to let those bastards have another shot at you. If Donovan can't make a case against them, what the hell. As long as they leave you alone, I don't give a damn what happens to them."

Wow. Masiela couldn't even find words to respond. He'd said yesterday that she'd *been* his life, the other part of him, and she'd believed him, but…*wow*.

After a long, tense moment, AJ managed a weak smile. "I'm going to remember this date a long time— the first time I ever saw Masiela Raquel Leal at a loss for words."

Her smile was lame, too. "I've just never seen you so committed to—" *To a woman. To me.* "—to nonaction.

You've always been the law-and-order, right-or-wrong, strict moral code guy."

"You expect me to sacrifice you just to see these guys punished?"

"Well, in my theoretical exercise, I survive." When he didn't respond immediately, she hesitantly went on. "It wouldn't be so difficult. We let them know where I am. If I'm right, one or more of them will show up here to kill me. And we—you, Detective Maricci, Detective Gadney—will be waiting."

AJ shook his head as he munched on the last brownie. "No way."

"The odds would be in our favor—four against three."

Stubbornly, he shook his head again. "Three cops plus an ex, against three dirty cops who won't care who gets in their way. They could take out half the neighborhood."

"Then we control the confrontation. You tell them I'm with you. Arrange for a handover at some out-of-the-way place where no civilians would be in danger."

"Convince them that I'm no better than they are." AJ muttered something she was probably better off not understanding.

She drew a breath to keep her voice calm. "It's been six years, Decker. People change. They're so damn arrogant they'll just think that you finally got smart, like them."

"*I* wouldn't buy me as a dirty cop. You think *they* would? They used to call me By-the-Book Decker, for God's sake."

"Convince them that a few pages have fallen out of the book." She knew he could do it; she'd seen him undercover before. He could make anyone believe anything.

He leaned toward her, his eyes flashing. "We're not using you as a target, Mas!"

"I *am* a target!"

His shrug was jerky. "Like you said, one they can't find. You wanna give them one they can find, let Donovan set himself up. He's got the same information you do, and he can get better protection. Let him risk his life to make the case."

"Yeah, well, I don't imagine he's anxious to do that."

"He doesn't have a death wish. Imagine that," AJ muttered.

"Let's talk to him." Masiela leaned toward him. "Donovan's a smart guy. He's seen this stuff. He's reached the same conclusion we have—we can get Rodriguez a new trial but we can't charge the cops. Let's ask his input."

For a long moment, AJ merely stared at her, his expression hard and forbidding, but not intimidating her in the least. Not when she knew it was motivated by concern for her. Then he picked up his cell from the table, scrolled to the number and pressed Send.

"Tell the secretary you're his old buddy from Georgia. It worked for Ty." She said it lightly, but didn't get even a faint smile from him.

He did as she suggested, though. Cradling her tea between her palms, she watched his face, trying to read something there. At first it was flat, nonexpressive, then his brow furrowed and something flashed through his eyes. The muscles in his jaw taut, he murmured the kind of words that encourage people to go on—"Really? Then what?"—then suddenly he disconnected.

Masiela's stomach knotted, as did her fingers on the glass. "What is it? What happened?"

"Donovan went to lunch today and never came back. His car's still in the parking garage, they found his cell phone in the gutter, and he missed court. He just vanished."

After a moment's stiff silence, he stood up and paced to the window, lifting the sheet a fraction of an inch to check out the quickly darkening sky. "Hell, Mas, you might get the chance to play target, after all."

Masiela swallowed hard. Sure, it'd been her suggestion, but it wasn't one she'd put a lot of thought into. It wasn't one she'd actually expected to carry out. People who set themselves up as targets were brave, had nerves of steel and were usually desperate. This evening she matched only one of the three.

Man up, she'd told AJ earlier. Looked like it was time for her to do the same.

"Worst case." Masiela came to stand beside AJ, and he automatically put his arm around her. It felt natural, he noticed. Like she belonged at his side. "Kinney and the others have kidnapped Donovan and have gotten, or are trying to get, my location from him."

"I don't see him standing up to their brand of persuasion. Donovan's a good prosecutor, but he's not a tough guy." His life had been pretty pampered. He wouldn't even know how to resist the sort of interrogation the detectives would put him through. "Maybe we should get the hell out of here."

"And go where?"

"We've got a nice clean jail. Immediate occupancy, no waiting."

"That's a temporary solution. You can't keep me locked up forever."

The idea held a certain appeal, enough to make him

grin briefly before taking out his cell again. "I sure as hell hope he's shacked up somewhere with a beautiful woman, and this is all for nothing," he muttered before the dispatcher answered. Even as he said it, he knew it wasn't possible. Donovan was the most ambitious man he knew. Nothing, not even the most beautiful woman in the world, would make him miss court.

A few phone calls later, he pulled Masiela down the hall and up the stairs with him. Letting go of her inside the bedroom, he kicked off his running shorts.

"Now?" she asked drily.

Grabbing a pair of denim shorts from the dresser, he held them out. "Help me get these on." When she complied, he took his pistol and a clip-on holster from the closet shelf and offered them to her. While she holstered the weapon, then attached it to his waistband, he pocketed two extra magazines.

His calls had been brief and discouraging. "Kinney, Myers and Taylor all called in sick today," he said grimly. "And Donovan's plane took off from the airstrip where he keeps it more than five hours ago. No flight plan; the guy can't be sure, but he thinks he had passengers."

AJ knew in his gut they'd headed east. If private plane had been the easiest, safest way to get Mas here, why not the same for his old friends?

His last call had been to Maricci. He and Gadney were on their way over.

With her own weapon clipped in place, they returned downstairs. All the lights were off in the front of the house—the rooms with uncovered windows—and he dimmed the lights in the kitchen, lessening the chances of casting a shadow on the makeshift curtains.

"How long did it take you and Donovan to get here?"

"About four hours, then another hour to drive from the airport."

AJ stared at the big window behind the couch. The others could already be in place in the woods out back. Had they brought Donovan to Copper Lake with them? Left him tied up inside the plane? Killed him? How desperate were they? Did they think they could kill Masiela and Donovan, then return to life as normal in Dallas? Arrogant, but possible. They would have set up an airtight alibi before they picked up Donovan. There were probably a dozen of Dallas's finest ready to swear on their honor that Myers, Kinney and Taylor had spent the entire weekend with them.

And they didn't intend to leave alive anyone who could say differently.

AJ's cell phone vibrated in his pocket, rattling against the extra magazines there. He fished it out and raised it to his ear.

"We just drove past your house," Maricci said. "Everything looks quiet. You want us inside, outside, in the woods, or what?"

"Why don't you take a walk through the woods?" AJ suggested. "Just be careful. You never know what kind of animals you might run into."

There was sound in the background, the engine cutting off, the bell dinging as the car door was opened. It stopped abruptly. "We're always careful in the woods around here."

AJ returned the phone to his pocket, then rummaged through the drawer of first one end table, then the other, before finding a compact flashlight. He handed it to Masiela and located another, heavier Maglite in the hall closet.

"I don't suppose you'd want to trade," she said drily,

holding up the lightweight one. "I always preferred steel to aluminum."

"Easier to break windows and heads, huh?" He switched with her, then went into the laundry room. She followed, closing the door behind her so the small room remained in the dark.

He lifted one edge of the curtain. The newly replaced security light brightly illuminated a portion of the yard; next door, at Pris's, another light did the same. Beyond that, though, were shadows, deepening until they blended into the moonless sky. A small army could be hidden back there, unseen as long as they remained still.

He smiled faintly. The problem was, the enemy couldn't achieve their goal if they stayed hidden in the woods. Sooner or later, they had to come to their target.

Reaching out, he found Mas's hand. Her skin was clammy, her fingers tightening for a moment around his. "You still like the idea of yourself as a target?"

She made an ugly face in the dim light. "I like the idea of ending this. Living scared is no fun."

Neither is dying. But he kept the comment to himself. She wasn't going to die tonight. He intended to make sure of that.

"If they get inside the house," he said grimly, "you get to the front room. Slide into that space behind the stack of Sheetrock. It's not much of a hiding place, but it's the best we've got."

She gave his fingers a particularly tight squeeze before releasing them and peeking through the curtain on her side. "I'm not hiding while you face them down, Decker. They want *me*."

"So do I," he retorted. "Alive and well."

She blinked at the fierceness of his response. He would

have given it a moment's thought himself, if every cop sense he had wasn't on alert, warning him that danger was near. "This is my town, Mas. My turf. I get paid the big bucks to protect the people in it."

"I've been trained by the best to do that, too."

It was true. She was far from the average victim: strong, smart, capable of defending herself. She'd never needed his protection when they were on the job together. Most people who'd messed with her had lived to regret it.

At the moment, he didn't care if Myers, Kinney and Taylor died regretting it.

He stared back where he knew the tree line was, still unable to make out any shapes in the shadows. Maricci and Gadney were back there now, dressed all in black for the job, wearing body armor and carrying high-powered rifles; and the Brat Pack were probably there, too, but AJ couldn't see a damn thing.

The first clue that something had changed came from next door: a high-pitched yapping from Pepper. A few seconds later, everything went dark: the security light, the thin strip of kitchen light coming under the door. Silence settled abruptly over the house as the refrigerator and the central air stopped.

Masiela swore, and he echoed it. "Come on," he whispered, grabbing her arm, pushing her toward the door. They'd seen enough. Now the action was starting.

"I won't hide—"

"If they're coming in, they're coming in the back. Let's get the hell away from the door."

They were halfway down the hall when breaking glass sounded in the laundry room. They quickened their steps, then AJ pushed her into the parlor and toward the pile of wallboard while he took up position at the door, pistol in his left hand.

An instant later, making only a whisper of sound, Masiela darted past him and into the living room across the hall. He swore silently. It had been too much to hope that she would hide as he asked.

Like him, she hovered just inside the opposite door, weapon in hand. She had the better vantage point; having to use his pistol in his off hand, he would have been too exposed if he'd taken that side. She didn't stay there, though. As floorboards creaked at the rear of the house, she gestured in the dim light coming through the windows, then disappeared. He wasn't sure if she intended to go through the dining room and circle around behind the intruders, or to ensure that none of them tried the same maneuver in reverse. He just knew that she was out of his sight. Out of range of any help he might give her.

A form appeared at the far end of the hall—broad-shouldered, well over six feet tall. Taylor. Behind him was another man, shorter, leaner. AJ listened hard, but couldn't hear a third set of footsteps. Had they left a guard outside, or was the other guy on a direct route to come face-to-face with Mas?

Shifting his weight until he was out of sight, AJ bit back hard on a groan as he fixed the flashlight into the awkward grip of his right hand. He stepped into place, switched on the beam and directed it and his pistol at the two men.

They froze just past the bathroom, Max Taylor in the lead, Stan Myers mostly concealed behind him. Taylor threw up one hand to shield his eyes, then grinned. "Hey, buddy. Long time no see."

"You should have made it longer," AJ said quietly. "I

don't remember inviting you into my house. That means it's okay if I shoot first and ask questions later."

"We don't have a problem with you, Decker." Myers's voice was cool, displaying no hint of fear, though he remained in the cover Taylor provided. "Just give us Leal, and we'll go away."

The way he said her name, the inflection, stirred a long-forgotten memory: Mas in the homicide division a week, maybe two; Kinney leering, making the other guys around laugh. *I hear she lives up to her name. Lay-all. Sleeps with anyone, everyone. You gonna be the first to do her in homicide, Decker? 'Cause if not, I wouldn't mind taking the job.*

AJ had blown him off—hadn't even dignified him with an answer. He should have stopped Kinney then, should have stood up for Mas then.

"You really think I'm stupid enough to believe you'll just take her and go?" AJ asked mildly.

"I'm not sure just how stupid you are, Deck. After all, you're hiding her."

"Yeah, you know about hiding, don't you? Why don't you come out from behind Taylor where I can get a good look at you?"

"That all you want?" Myers asked with a sneer.

"A good look, a good shot." AJ shrugged. "Doesn't matter. With the load I've got in this pistol, I can take out both you and your shield with one shot."

Taylor stepped to the side, his back to the wall to keep Myers in the open. "'You go first, Taylor,'" he muttered, mimicking his bud. "'I'll be right behind you.' Yeah, hiding like a damn coward behind me."

AJ's right fingers were starting to cramp, making the light waver. "Mas and I were just talking about that, how him and Kinney always manage to bring up the rear.

It's a wonder they haven't gotten you killed before this, Taylor."

Distantly, AJ heard a swish. The door between the kitchen and dining room swinging open? He would give damn near anything to know exactly where Masiela was, what she was planning. She was an expert shot and could do some serious damage with the flashlight—or with her bare hands and feet, if necessary. Still, good cops could get unlucky or taken by surprise.

"Enough talk, Deck. We didn't come all this way to screw around with you. Taylor here might have second thoughts about killing you, but me, I don't much care. I always thought you were a sanctimonious prick anyway. Hell, I should've let that scumbag kill you when I had the chance."

A knot settled in AJ's gut. How much of his misplaced loyalty to these guys had been based on Myers's saving his life all those years ago? And the bastard wished he hadn't done it. Intended to finish what he'd stopped back then.

AJ's arm was throbbing. Any minute now, the flashlight was going to slip from his fingers, no matter how hard he tried to hold it. In the dark, Myers and Taylor would scatter, taking cover in the living room or retreating to the kitchen. They could trap Masiela between them.

He sighted the pistol, grateful for all those hours spent practicing at the firing range with both his dominant and his off hands, and squeezed the trigger at the same instant he dropped the light. The blast rattled the walls and was followed almost instantly by a grunt, a body slumping to the floor, a curse.

"Damn sonovabitch shot me!" Myers gritted out. "Kill the bastard and find Leal!"

Though she'd prepared herself for gunfire, the first shot sent a jolt through Masiela. She pressed her spine tight against the unfinished wall in the dining room, pistol gripped in both hands, and inched toward the kitchen door. It had opened once, barely a few inches, the space filled by a shadow that must have been Dave Kinney, before it melted back into the kitchen and the door swung shut. Likely, he'd gone toward the hall to help out his buddies. She knew how they thought: no woman could possibly be as good as they were. Their priority now was taking out the real danger—Decker— then killing her would be practically an afterthought.

She never had liked the way they thought.

As more shots sounded in the hallway, she eased up to the door, listening, hearing shuffling sounds from the other side. She couldn't identify who or where, though. Taking a deep breath, she wrapped her stiff fingers around the knob, turned it carefully, then pulled the door open one agonizing inch at a time. Nothing appeared out of place in the kitchen. The gunshots were coming from somewhere to her right, just outside the kitchen door and, it seemed, farther down the hall in the library. If Myers was still in the hall, down—dying?—that meant Taylor was likely in the library. As long as their attention was focused on the hall and AJ, she had the advantage—she hoped—of surprise.

She squeezed through the doorway. A shape too solidly black to be shadow was hunkered near the hall door, back to her. Dave Kinney, in the flesh. Anger swept through her, leaving ice in its wake. A fellow cop, whose job was to serve and protect and be better than the average citizen. A liar, a deceiver, a murderer. For years she'd detested him. At that moment she hated him—for what he'd done, for what he was. It would be so easy to kill him—justifiable, even. He was shooting at a police officer, and not just any officer, but Decker, his old friend, his fellow cop. She could use whatever force was necessary to stop him.

Her arm was rock steady as she took aim center mass. She'd practiced for this—close range, distance, head shots, body shots. Kill shots. Practiced until she was perfect, until she could practically do it blindfolded, until the process was second nature, but in all her years as a cop, she'd never had to take that shot.

She'd never imagined that the first time she shot a man, it would be in the back. *Never* imagined it would be a cop.

"Come on, Decker," Kinney called after a momentary silence. "You can't outlast us. We came prepared."

Masiela strained to hear something from the direction of the parlor—movement, panting, swearing. For an instant her heart pounded, then AJ's voice, quiet and calm, sounded.

"Backup will be here any minute."

"A bunch of small-town cops, never been shot at in their lives," Kinney scoffed. "We'll kill them, too."

AJ was right, Masiela realized. So was Kinney. By now someone would have called for help—Maricci or Gadney, one of the neighbors. More cops, more guns, more danger. They could take out half the neighborhood, AJ had warned earlier.

Or half the police department.

Her finger was tightening on the trigger, slow steady pressure, when a sound, boots crunching on glass, came from the direction of the laundry room. Kinney heard it, too, abruptly pivoting in that direction, firing off a rapid burst of shots. There was a stumble, a crash, a groan, a panicked whisper: *"Ty!"*

Masiela stepped away from the wall, readjusted her aim and pulled the trigger. The blast propelled Kinney sideways, carrying him into the wall, where he slumped to the floor. Unlike Myers and Gadney, he didn't swear or groan. He lay silent, unmoving. Dead, she hoped.

"Two of your buds are down, Taylor," she said loudly. "You want to come out, or do you wanna be next?"

Into the long silence that followed came the wail of distant sirens. A "shots fired" call at a police officer's home would bring out every cop in town and every deputy in the county. "You've got about a minute to decide," she warned Taylor.

"You want to die, big guy, I'd be happy to accommodate you." Maricci's voice came from the left, moving stealthily toward the library. Mas saw what must have made up Taylor's mind for him an instant later: the red dot of a laser sight centered on his chest.

"Okay, okay, I'm coming out." Taylor's weapon hit the floor, then his shadow loomed in the doorway.

Maricci shoved him to the floor and cuffed him, then spoke into the mic on his shoulder, calling for paramedics.

Sirens blared then silenced, and doors slammed outside. Blue lights lit up the night, flashing through the front windows, as she went down the hall. She supplemented it with her flashlight, pausing a safe distance from Myers. He was bleeding, unconscious, but still breathing. Maricci came toward them with a pair of Flex-cuf restraints, and she stepped over the man and the blood pool and shined the light ahead of her. "AJ? AJ, where are you?"

She directed the beam into the parlor and saw his feet first. Flip-flops—not the footwear of choice for a gun battle. That would go in the teasing-for-the-rest-of-their-lives category, along with that godawful Hawaiian shirt.

He was sitting on the floor just inside the doorway, his back to the wall. Wallboard dust from a couple of too-close shots had turned his black cast white, along with an unused magazine resting in his lap.

"Hey, Mas," he said, his voice quiet, subdued. "Help me up, will you? I can't seem to get my feet under me."

"Too much excitement on top of a broken wrist, huh? You never did get the adrenaline rush like the rest of us." She set the flashlight aside, holstered her pistol, then bent to hook her arm under his. As she leaned close, the house lights came on again, and she found herself just inches from a red blot on his shirt, wet and growing bigger. She touched it, convinced it couldn't be what it appeared, and her fingers came away sticky.

Dear God, he'd been shot.

The emergency room was always busy on Saturday nights, but AJ had never seen it like this. Multiple gunshot victims, plus one badly beaten Donovan, recovered from the trunk of the bastards' rental car, just about every relative Ty Gadney had, along with most of the Deckers within driving distance, and so many cops that it looked like a convention. Considering he'd been shot, the trauma surgeon had told him he was the least of their worries that night. No threat to his life, no surgery.

Considering he'd been shot, AJ reflected, he felt pretty damn good. It didn't matter much if the Texas courts took on the case against Myers and Taylor. They'd tried to kill three cops and a lawyer in Georgia. Georgia wasn't letting them go for a hell of a long time.

And *he* wasn't letting Mas go. Even if that meant going back to Texas with her.

He eased up in the bed, testing the pain in his shoulder and arm. They'd packed the wound, put him in a sling and made noise about keeping him overnight. There was broken glass, splintered wood, Sheetrock and blood all over his house. He had no problem with spending the night elsewhere.

He was swinging his feet over the side of the bed to the floor, when Maricci came into the cubicle, caught him under the ankles and swept both legs back onto the mattress. For good measure, he also locked the side rails up.

"What do you need?"

"Where's Mas?"

"She's talking to Ray Donovan a couple doors down. He's not feeling real macho right now—letting his guard down, giving her up."

AJ shook his head. "They beat the crap out of him. Anyone would have talked eventually."

"You wouldn't," Maricci replied. "I'm not sure she would have. She's tough."

"More than you know."

"I'll tell her you want to talk to her," Maricci said on his way out.

Talk? Mostly what he wanted to do was hold her. Look at her. Make sure she was all right. Touch her and just be with her. They hadn't had more than a couple minutes together since she'd realized he'd been shot.

The curtain that enclosed his cubicle fluttered, then Masiela slipped inside. Her hair was down, any makeup she might have put on in the past forty-eight hours was long gone, and her clothes were dusty and dotted with blood.

She looked more amazingly beautiful than he'd ever seen her.

She tugged the curtains shut behind her, then came to his right side. Her fingers were cool against his skin as she bent to rest her arms on the railing. "You want an update, I guess. Kinney, of course, is dead. I shot him. Myers isn't dead. You should have shot him again. Gadney was hit in the leg; he just got out of surgery and is fine. Donovan...I don't know what they did to him, but they kept him coherent enough to fly them here. They planned to kill him as soon as they got back. He's pretty closed off. Doesn't want to talk to anyone. His parents are flying in on their private jet tonight. As soon as Dr. Cate says he can go, they're whisking him off someplace." She paused. "Have I left anyone out?"

"You." He tried to take her hand, but the best he could manage was brushing the back of his fingers against hers. "Are you okay?"

Her eyes grew darker, and she gazed at the curtains that blocked her view, down in the last cubicle, of Dave Kinney's body. After a moment, she met AJ's gaze again. "I didn't want to kill him, but the choice was his."

Her answer was simple, thoughtful, reasonable. He liked it. It was no more than he'd thought the first time he'd killed a subject. No less than he'd expected from her.

"So what are your plans?"

She blinked, then tucked a strand of hair back. "I haven't really had time to think."

"I have. Put that railing down and climb up here with me." He carefully moved to the edge of the bed, making room for her to stretch out next to him. The instant she came close enough for him to feel her heat, to smell her scent, tension he'd hardly noticed disappeared.

She rested her head on his good shoulder, and he held her the best he could with his casted arm. "So you've been thinking…" she prompted.

"I have."

"Solved the world's problems?"

"I don't give a damn about the world's problems. Just yours and mine." His gaze locked with hers. "I figured out one thing for sure. I want you in my life, Mas. All these years, that's what's been missing—why I haven't fallen in love, gotten married, had kids, been satisfied. I needed you to do those things, but I was too stubborn to see it."

"I'm still a lawyer," she pointed out.

"Yeah, well, we could use a few more honest lawyers."

"And cops."

"Absolutely."

She gazed at him, her fingers lightly touching his throat, his jaw, his cheek. "So…you think you might need to marry me? Have kids with me? Be satisfied with me?"

"I don't think it. I know."

"My job's in Dallas."

"I lived there once. I can do it again." He grinned. "I know for a fact that Dallas PD will be looking for a few experienced detectives."

"I've lived there a long time. Maybe it's time for *me* to try someplace else."

AJ's muscles tightened. He would go back to Texas and be happy, though deep inside there was a part of him that preferred the slower pace of Copper Lake. The events of the night aside, it was a safer place. Home to good friends who would risk their lives for a woman they didn't even know. Close to his family. A good town to raise kids and a great house for them—once the new repairs were added to the old.

"My parents travel a lot and don't have much time for me when they're home," she went on, talking softly, as if to herself. "The twins live halfway across the state, and no matter how good our intentions are, we still don't see each other often. It's doubtful that if I got shot back home, anyone would even show up at the hospital, unless my grandmothers managed to escape the retirement home for a few hours." She looked up, eyes wide. "There are Deckers all over the waiting room."

"We tend to stick close to home. I think I was the first one in six generations to move further than two hours away for more than a few years." He hesitated, then referred back to a comment she made earlier. "I've got a large enough family that the kids wouldn't notice if anyone's missing from their mother's family."

She pressed her face against his chest, and her arms tightened around his ribcage. "But you'd leave them for Dallas."

"For you."

"What about your house? What about that amazing library I put so much work into?"

"We could find another house in Dallas, with a better library."

She snorted at the thought. Probably rightly so. He didn't know what kind of money she made, but he knew what he could earn in Texas, and it wouldn't get them anywhere near the house he had now.

"There's an assistant DA out there, along with everyone else, who mentioned that there's going to be an opening in the DA's office soon. You know, for a long time I wanted to be a prosecutor. Do you think I could handle it?"

AJ figured she could handle damn near anything. Like Maricci said, she was tough—and she was making him feel pretty damn weak. "Can we nail down all the details later, Mas? Right now there's just one thing I need to know from you."

She smiled smugly. "Yes, I'll marry you."

"Okay, make that two."

Levering up on one arm, she gazed at him. "You want me to say it first, don't you?"

"You always did have that thing about leading." Her hair fell over his right hand, and he knotted his fingers in its cool silk. "I don't care about first. You've been the most important woman in my life since the day we met in the lieutenant's office. You came into my house and made me feel at home. You make me want things I was pretty sure I never wanted. Hell, you make me crazy. I can't stand the idea of not being with you. I love you, Mas."

There was a sheen to her eyes that he'd never seen before: tears. He'd brought the strongest, toughest woman he'd ever known to tears, and in a good way. She moistened her lips, but before she could speak, someone else did.

"In case you're not aware, you have a rather large audience out here," Cate called from outside the curtain. "If you'd rather finish this conversation in private, we'll have a room for you in about five minutes."

There were a few groans, followed by a disgruntled comment. "You never were any fun, Cate."

Masiela stared down at him, and he knew just what she saw. No flush, no embarrassment, just the serious steady look of the man who'd saved her life and would do it again, in both small ways and large. The man who would give up his family, his home and his job to be with her. The man she would do the same for.

She lifted herself until they were nose to nose, intense hazel gaze to intense dark gaze, and whispered, "You make me crazy, too, Decker. And I've loved you longer than any self-respecting woman would admit to. Loved you, love you, will always love you. Details don't matter. You and me—that's all that matters."

She kissed him then, gentleness quickly giving way to hunger and greed and pure lust. As the kiss—the woman—went to his head, he was dimly aware of those voices again.

"What did she say?"

"Whispering's not fair. We got to hear everything he said."

Then the fluttering of the curtain was followed by a familiar voice. His mother sounded quite pleased with herself when she said, "I'm going to be a mother-in-law! Go on now, get away from here. Leave my son and the woman who loves him alone."

* * * * *

Be sure to pick up next month's
COVERT CHRISTMAS, a 3-in-1
from Silhouette Romantic Suspense,
featuring OPEN SEASON,
an original novella by Marilyn Pappano.
Available September 28, 2010.

COMING NEXT MONTH

Available September 28, 2010

SRSCNM0910

REQUEST YOUR FREE BOOKS!

2 FREE NOVELS PLUS 2 FREE GIFTS!

ROMANTIC SUSPENSE

Sparked by Danger, Fueled by Passion.

YES! Please send me 2 FREE Silhouette® Romantic Suspense novels and my 2 FREE gifts (gifts are worth about $10). After receiving them, if I don't wish to receive any more books, I can return the shipping statement marked "cancel." If I don't cancel, I will receive 4 brand-new novels every month and be billed just $4.24 per book in the U.S. or $4.99 per book in Canada. That's a saving of 15% off the cover price! It's quite a bargain! Shipping and handling is just 50¢ per book.* I understand that accepting the 2 free books and gifts places me under no obligation to buy anything. I can always return a shipment and cancel at any time. Even if I never buy another book from Silhouette, the two free books and gifts are mine to keep forever.

240/340 SDN E5Q4

Name	(PLEASE PRINT)	
Address		Apt. #
City	State/Prov.	Zip/Postal Code

Signature (if under 18, a parent or guardian must sign)

Mail to the Silhouette Reader Service:

IN U.S.A.: P.O. Box 1867, Buffalo, NY 14240-1867
IN CANADA: P.O. Box 609, Fort Erie, Ontario L2A 5X3

Not valid for current subscribers to Silhouette Romantic Suspense books.

Want to try two free books from another line?
Call 1-800-873-8635 or visit www.morefreebooks.com.

* Terms and prices subject to change without notice. Prices do not include applicable taxes. N.Y. residents add applicable sales tax. Canadian residents will be charged applicable provincial taxes and GST. Offer not valid in Quebec. This offer is limited to one order per household. All orders subject to approval. Credit or debit balances in a customer's account(s) may be offset by any other outstanding balance owed by or to the customer. Please allow 4 to 6 weeks for delivery. Offer available while quantities last.

Your Privacy: Silhouette is committed to protecting your privacy. Our Privacy Policy is available online at www.eHarlequin.com or upon request from the Reader Service. From time to time we make our lists of customers available to reputable third parties who may have a product or service of interest to you. If you would prefer we not share your name and address, please check here. ☐

Help us get it right—We strive for accurate, respectful and relevant communications. To clarify or modify your communication preferences, visit us at www.ReaderService.com/consumerschoice.

SRS10R

*See below for a sneak peek at
our inspirational line, Love Inspired®.
Introducing HIS HOLIDAY BRIDE
by bestselling author Jillian Hart*

Autumn Granger gave her horse rein to slide toward the town's new sheriff.

"Hey, there." The man in a brand-new Stetson, black T-shirt, jeans and riding boots held up a hand in greeting. He stepped away from his four-wheel drive with "Sheriff" in black on the doors and waded through the grasses. "I'm new around here."

"I'm Autumn Granger."

"Nice to meet you, Miss Granger. I'm Ford Sherman, from Chicago." He knuckled back his hat, revealing the most handsome face she'd ever seen. Big blue eyes contrasted with his sun-tanned complexion.

"I'm guessing you haven't seen much open land. Out here, you've got to keep an eye on cows or they're going to tear your vehicle apart."

"What?" He whipped around. Sure enough, mammoth black-and-white creatures had started to gnaw on his four-wheel drive. They clustered like a mob, mouths and tongues and teeth bent on destruction. One cow tried to pry the wiper off the windshield, another chewed on the side mirror. Several leaned through the open window, licking the seats.

"Move along, little dogie." He didn't know the first thing about cattle.

The entire herd swiveled their heads to study him curiously. Not a single hoof shifted. The animals soon returned to chewing, licking, digging through his possessions.

Autumn laughed, a warm and wonderful sound. "Thanks,

I needed that." She then pulled a bag from behind her saddle and waved it at the cows. "Look what I have, guys. Cookies."

Cows swung in her direction, and dozens of liquid brown eyes brightened with cookie hopes. As she circled the car, the cattle bounded after her. The earth shook with the force of their powerful hooves.

"Next time, you're on your own, city boy." She tipped her hat. The cowgirl stayed on his mind, the sweetest thing he had ever seen.

*Will Ford be able to stick it out in the country
to find out more about Autumn?
Find out in HIS HOLIDAY BRIDE
by bestselling author Jillian Hart,
available in October 2010
only from Love Inspired®.*